CLARI

MW01716259

AUGUST 2021 - ISSUE 179

## FICTION



## NON-FICTION



Neil Clarke: Publisher/Editor-in-Chief
Sean Wallace: Editor
Kate Baker: Non-Fiction Editor/Podcast Director

Clarkesworld Magazine (ISSN: 1937-7843) • Issue 179 • August 2021


www.clarkesworldmagazine.com

# Candide; Life-

BETH GODER

Seva is waiting for Jal in the eggnog eatery where they had their first date. A moving rainbow of eggnog mini-cups streams past on a conveyor belt. She grabs a birthday cake nog, removing the cup from underneath the safety dome. The aroma triggers an access request in her microenvironment, which she grants. The smell of sugar, milk, and chocolate engulfs her. Even though she had cake for breakfast (leftovers from her nineteenth birthday party), she wants more. It's her policy that you can never have too much cake.

Seva sets her microenvironment to play the Overture to *Candide* on loop. The intensity of the first few measures is a roar that lifts her entire body. She conducts compulsively, her arm twitching in time to the music; she doesn't care who sees her. When the main theme comes in, that soaring melody that runs up against the frenetic pace of the whole but is never swallowed, her heart feels like it is transcending her chest. This is music!

The third time through, she makes an emotion capture.

*::Candide; joy-*

The capture isn't professional quality, not artwork or anything of value, but she's still happy she made it. It doesn't have to be good. Her use to society is in creating music, not emotion captures. That's how she claimed a spot at university. Musicians, her mother says, will always be needed, because digital mechanisms can't reproduce music with the correct level of emotion. Her goal is to become a symphonic percussionist in a city with a population of at least seventy thousand.

She reviews *::Candide; joy-*. Clearly, it needs work. The capture contains her soaring emotions, and the Overture itself could never disappoint, but the sound of the eggnog conveyor belt is perceptible, and she neglected to imagine a visual. The eye view is simply the default blue.

*I should just garbage it*, she thinks. Send it to delete ops who will take it off her implants and her backup storage and hunt it down from any digi-worms that have already grabbed it, and maybe even pull it out of her perma-memory file if the rumors are true. But *::Candide; joy-* contains this one pure moment, so for reasons she can't explain, she tucks it up into her nova-storage.

She swipes a spicy shrimp eggnog, and then a multicolored nog with the disconcerting title "best seeds." Forty minutes and five nogs later, Seva wonders if Jal is ghosting her, but as she's tossing her last cup into the dilator, Jal runs in.

"I've got to show you something," he says, without preamble or apology for being late. His hair sticks up like a wave, and his implants are set to make the tips glow. A fitted shirt hangs over precisely ripped jeans. He wears a ring on every finger, and two on each thumb. Real rings, not digitally imaged.

Seva wishes she had downloaded a new bracelet mod. He already saw the floating triangles when they jumped into the neon pond by Calooki Woods on their second date, but it's too late to change now.

He grabs her hand, which feels a little like listening to the first measures of the Overture to *Candide*. She pushes down her breath. "You're late."

He asks if it's cool if they go back to his workshop, because he wants to show her his newest sculpture. He's been working on it for months, and she'll be the first one to see it in its completed form. Her bracelet triangles shimmer all the way up her arm, responding to her spike of adrenaline. She digitally slams off the emotion mod, but not quickly enough. It's so obvious that her heart is pounding.

She triggers her auto-pay to settle her bill before they both dash out to the street.

They wind their way through downtown. Her microenvironment automatically blocks the smog. The city is like a chaotic percussion section, all crashes and footsteps and the staccato notes of voices, but she never mutes ambient sound. The city makes its own sort of music.

An art reveal is something special, even better than the night sky simulator they did for their third date, which was super romantic. She's only known him for three months, but maybe they have the potential to create something of value, like a relationship contract or a joint artistic project.

They hop into a transport pod. His hand is still clutching hers. She puts her head against his shoulder, and he slips his arm around her, bringing her into the intensity of his warmth.

• • •

Jal's workshop is jammed into one of the university's buildings, partitioned to the exact millimeter. Tools line the walls in neat rows. A scraggly broom rests in the corner. An orange couch is smooshed against the wall.

The center of the room is hidden by a privi-screen, the molecules jumping around so it's impossible to see whatever lies behind.

Jal picks up the broom, even though the floor is spotless. He sweeps imaginary dust, then sweeps again.

"Okay," he says, with an indrawn breath, pushing the broom back into the corner.

The privi-screen dissipates.

What lies behind it is a sculpture of a feminine arm. The limestone has been carved with precision. The hand stretches out, the fingers slightly curved—a beautiful portrayal of motion, made with skill and patience.

There is something that bothers her about this disembodied arm. Why has he chosen a female body part as the medium of his artistic expression? And, what's more, this arm is disconcertingly familiar, with its bent elbow. Seva looks down at her own arm. She bends her elbow. Is the sculpture based on her body? But how can she tell? An arm is an arm. It's not, on its own, a particularly distinctive limb.

Jal bounces on his toes, eager for her response. The need for approval is like a physical presence in the room, even though he tries to hide behind a nonchalant expression.

"It's amazing," she says, pushing aside her thoughts about gender and power and the choices of artists.

"That's not everything." He guides her closer, one hand on her back. She reaches out to touch the arm, which is so similar to her own. An access request pings. She gasps.

He's embedded an emotion capture within the sculpture. Gingerly, she allows the emotion capture to take over her senses. She expected something like *::Generic; happy-* or *::Generic; strong emotional discovery-*, but what she experiences is more. He's created his own emotion capture, built it himself, and embedded it into the sculpture. The experience is three quick breaths, aching sorrow, the hand reaching out to you, the hand that will never reach you. There is a lingering ghostly quality, which is enhanced by the visual of the sculpture.

Although she can appreciate Jal's effort, she can see the roughness of the piece. The transitions are shaky. The emotional resonance loses its force after the third second. It's okay, but not a masterpiece. Jal's no Salavonic, but who could rival *::Singular raindrop falls on back of wet bird-* or *::Violinist collapses onstage-*?

Seva comes back to herself, the residuals of the capture drifting away, until there is only Jal by her side, and the sculpture in front of her.

"I didn't know you were specializing in multimedia," she says.

He seems dissatisfied by her response. "I'm not. But the university allows for experimentation." He looks back at the sculpture, then at her, vulnerability twisting in his face, the beginnings of a fragile anger.

Quickly, she praises the piece, commenting on the merging of the physical sculpture and digital emotion, which she really did think was well done. Some critics would argue that reliance on multimedia diminishes the power of an emotion capture as an art form, but Seva thinks there is potential in these combinations. Creativity, she knows, often comes from the merging of two disparate things.

After his desire for praise is sated, Jal has a lot to say about emotion captures. They spend the next hour debating the benefits of sensory deprivation as a technique for emotional enhancement and geeking out about the work of Salavonic. It's the sort of conversation without pauses. They both have so much to say.

"I made something, too," Seva says, caught up in the enthusiasm of their conversation. "Not art," she adds quickly. "Just something I felt today." She pulls up *::Candide; joy-*, debating whether she should share access.

"You make emotion captures, too?" Somehow, the timbre of their conversation changes, the excitement leaking out. Jal's voice is neutral, but she senses something behind it.

"Not art," she says again. "Just for fun." Maybe this was a bad idea. "Never mind."

"I want to see it."

She wants to explain that creating an emotion capture, for her, is like playing a string of sixty-fourth notes, which you can only do if you are concentrating very hard or not thinking about it at all. Instead, before she has time to lose her nerve, she sends him the access code to *::Candide; joy-*.

His face, while he experiences the emotion capture, is animated with delight. This is a type of vulnerability, she realizes, this ability to see someone else having an emotional experience, even if the origin of those emotions come from without. She wonders what she looked like while viewing his sculpture, if her face twitched at the ghostly sadness of the hand reaching out.

When the emotion capture ends, Jal comes back to himself. Now the emotions flitting across his face are his own, and she can't read them. He is silent for too long.

"It's not art," she says again. "It's just how I feel. How music makes me feel."

"You shouldn't garbage it," he says. "I mean, there's some interesting stuff in there. It's not a terrible beginner's piece."

The words are like a blow, but worse is the shame she feels at her reaction. He's just saying what's true, what she's said to herself.

She forces herself to laugh. "The music is good, though."

"Yeah, it's a good recording." Jal pauses. "Have you shown this to anyone else?"

"I just made it this afternoon. Really quickly."

"I'm just saying this so you don't get hurt. Maybe don't let anyone else see it, okay?"

Suddenly, she wants him to see her doing what she's good at, her real art. "You should come to my concert this week." She pings him with tickets. "I have a xylophone solo."

"It's a difficult medium," he says. What she hears is: we can't all be artists.

It's three weeks before she visits Jal's work space again. It's a quick stop on the way to the dance plaza, where they're meeting some friends. In typical Jal fashion, he's left one of his projects until the last minute, so he needs to crank out a sketch of a vase in twenty minutes.

While he's working, Seva wanders the workshop. Her microenvironment keeps out the limestone dust. She avoids the arm sculpture, which still unsettles her, despite the beauty of those upturned fingers.

In the corner, there's a hunk of limestone, half-sculpted. She can't tell what it's going to be. Maybe a flame or a rooster. Jal once told her that sculpting is about removing the stone that isn't supposed to be there, bit by bit, until the true thing emerges. It's the opposite of music, which is about filling the silence with the notes that are meant to exist. She muses on this dichotomy in art—subtraction and addition, removal and creation, the full and empty spaces.

She touches the flame/rooster thing, and it pings her with an access request. Jal never locks anything in his workshop. With a start, she realizes he is creating another multimedia project. She shouldn't look in on this half-created thing, but she's curious.

The emotion capture that engulfs her seems to be a meditation on art, the path of the artist. The male figure, a sculptor, emerges in heroic form. Seva bites back a laugh. It's clearly meant to be Jal. His story is outlined in quick snatches of feeling—the struggle of the artist, the intensity of his craft, the complexity of his art. Is this really how he sees himself? The budding genius?

When the first notes of Overture to *Candide* play, all the laughter drains from Seva's body. The soaring emotion she feels is her own, distorted, thrown back at her. He's taken *::Candide; joy-* and incorporated it into his emotion capture. Stolen it. Twisted it. Claimed it as his own. The male artist bows, full of glory, lifted up by the emotion of *::Candide; joy-*.

She slams off the access point.

Jal is hunched over a stencil. His implants are projecting patterns onto the physical paper. The vase is coming along nicely.

"What is that?" says Seva. The rage in her voice causes him to jump.

"A vase?" he says, then sees she is pointing at the half-finished sculpture. With a wave of his hand, the stencils disappear. He's taken off his rings to draw, and his hands look strangely vulnerable without them. "It's not finished yet. I'm still tinkering." He doesn't even realize why she's angry.

"When I shared my emotion capture with you, that was just for you. Not for you to cannibalize into some narrative about yourself." She hadn't even known he was making a copy. This betrayal congeals in the pit of her stomach.

"Everything that happens to me fuels my art." He strikes the same heroic pose as the male figure in the emotion capture, ready to take on the role of the persecuted artist. Has he practiced this pose in the mirror?

"You took what I made. It's not your art." The moment crystallizes in front of her. What she says next is as much for herself as it is for him. "It's mine."

He snorts. "Do I have to give the stone credit, too?"

For the first time, she looks at him objectively—his stylized hair, the precisely ripped jeans, the commitment to living as if everyone should acknowledge him as a great artist. She chisels away at her image of him, until the truth emerges.

When she first showed him *::Candide; joy-*, he was, she realizes now, angry. It's not that her emotion capture was especially good. It's that she dared to make it. She feels there is a part of Jal that wants her to crumple and shrink, like the stone he shapes.

She could take one of his precisely arranged tools and hammer the flame/rooster statue until it turns to dust. She could ask him to destroy the stolen emotion capture, but she knows that Jal will never be able to use it properly, and he'll never be able to reproduce anything like it.

Instead, she says, "Do you think you'll ever make anything of worth?"

This question, so invasive and piercing, causes him to flinch. It is the question all artists ask themselves in dark, quiet moments. At its core, unanswerable.

His mouth opens and shuts as he tries to gather himself enough to answer.

Seva instructs her microenvironment to block out his form, his voice. Suddenly, it is as if she is alone in the workshop. Whatever answer he gives is erased. One by one, she scrubs out his sculptures from her view.

Without another word, she leaves.

Seva spends two angry hours in the eggnog place, blocking out all outside noise from her microenvironment. She plays a game called "No More Cows," which requires her to roll a giant ball of milk droplets, picking up random items to make the ball bigger. The loss condition is picking up a cow. When she accidently falls into a pit of cows on the fifth level, she rage-quits the game.

Instead of starting another game, she pulls up Salavonic's *::Singular raindrop falls on back of wet bird-*

A bird, huddled under fir needles, alive in heartbeats. The beat of rain. In the moment before flight, one raindrop touches the bird, working softly into her feathers. That moment before flight, this small life, so full of wonder, so close to death.

The practice room is quiet. With xylophone mallets in hand, Seva plays a recording of Overture to *Candide*. As she listens, she makes an emotion capture, the flow of the music interspersed with the movement of her life. When the xylophone part comes, her intense focus is matched only by the precision of her notes. She plays, swept up by the music. The moments of her life bleed into the work, creating an experience that is full of her memories and thoughts and feelings.

After, as she plays back the emotion capture, she realizes Jal is absent from her story. Excised, as if he never existed.

She doesn't know what to name this multimedia thing she's made, this emotion capture paired with music, so she finds a digital program to scan for a possible title. What comes back is this:

*::Is our only worth in what we make?-*

This is a question she's thought about for a long time, but it's not something she can answer. The program must have picked up on her thoughts.

She rejects the title. Instead, she makes her own:

*::Candide; life-*

She likes the simplicity of this title. The Overture to *Candide* itself is buzzing with life, but it's her life too that's interwoven into the piece, her thoughts and feelings, her perseverance, her doubts.

Exhausted, she pulls the xylophone cover over the instrument and places the mallets in her stick bag. Before she closes the emotion capture, she saves the file with her name. She hesitates, then, before she can lose her nerve, she uploads *::Candide; life-*, sending what she's made out into the world.

## ABOUT THE AUTHOR

**Beth Goder** works as an archivist, processing the papers of economists, scientists, and other interesting folks. Her fiction has appeared in venues such as *Escape Pod, Fireside,* and *Flash Fiction Online.*

# A Thousand Tiny Gods

## NADIA AFIFI

The minister's wife arrives at the Bahrain Ministry of Nanotechnology in a black limousine with dark, tinted windows. She normally eschews the hijab, but today, she's wrapped in a black abaya with a full face covering, a useful method of concealing her identity without drawing attention from those who would question her presence here, of all places. Under her veil, her head turns left and right, scanning her surroundings, before she gathers her skirts and strolls into the building.

I stand with crossed arms at the second-story window with other nanotech developers, jostling for the best view. Animated voices surround me, the air thick with excitement and strong coffee.

"Think any of her security team will leak the story?"

"She wouldn't be stupid enough to let that happen. Doesn't she have three degrees?"

"Maybe she wants to be caught. Cause a scandal and embarrass the minister."

"Her husband hates nanotech, like half of the country. He'd shut us down if he could."

"Well, she hates her husband, doesn't she? She'd be crazy not to."

I slip away, gossip about anti-nanotech protestors and robotic mistresses trailing in my wake. My heels click on the tiled floor. Like most Bahraini programmers, I normally wear a uniform of worn jeans and a faded T-shirt from some obscure Arab metal band. Today is different. I need to convey power, professionalism, seriousness—all that noise that developers usually tune out, lost in the realm of zeroes and ones.

The clothes work their magic—I feel different today. I began my morning with a run along the new elevated corniche on the western side of the island, watching the daily supercavitational shuttle to Saudi Arabia tear across the water. Ate a za'atar and olive oil manaqish from the food stand in the lobby, put flavored hazelnut syrup in my coffee. Walked to work, taking advantage of an unusual cold front. On hotter mornings, I swim in the canal that runs through the condos on the northern tip of Bahrain, reserved for government workers. It's a good life—I can climb down from my back patio directly into the water and swim between the kayaks and lazy riverboats, popular with young Bahrainis. I pay all my bills and order takeout twice a week.

But I can do better. And today, at last, the perfect opportunity has arrived.

"Assign me to the minister's wife's case," I say without preamble, strolling into Dr. Jawad's office. His eyes narrow as I lean back on his visitor's chair, propping my crossed legs on his desk. My heels are red, the color of power. Or so I heard on some podcast.

"She has a name, you know," the doctor says. He taps his feet with unconcealed impatience. His fingers scroll over the 3D holo-monitor in the center of his desk, pulling up patient files with no regard for privacy.

"I know," I say. "Mrs. Zainab Bint Hassan al-Mansouri. Aged sixty-one. First wife to the Minister of Defense and Veterans Affairs. Worked for the same ministry after graduating from Cambridge. See, doc? I can do basic research. And I can do more than basic programming. I've proven as much. As an added bonus, I'm the only woman on the team, and don't you think this case needs a woman's touch? This educated, modern lady would probably be more encouraged to see a woman as one of the main faces handling her care, leading the team. It'll be great press."

I deliver this pitch a little too fast, my nervousness getting the best of me. But I can see the grudging effect of my words on the senior doctor. He takes in my professional, well-tailored attire, perhaps mulling the optics of the situation. But he's not ready to concede yet.

"Aren't you the head of the Cosmetics nanotech team, Manal?" Dr. Jawad counters. "I don't know what Mrs. Mansouri wants yet, but I suspect it's more than some skin treatments. Rumors are that she has cancer."

"Meaning I'm perfect for the job." I grab a donut, peppered with rainbow sprinkles, from the box on his desk and hide my irritation behind a hearty bite. It's been two years since I was moved from Preventative Medicine to Cosmetic Enhancements, but I still feel the sting, sharp like salty water on raw skin. It wasn't for lack of ability. I coded the main logic—with Dr. Jawad, no less—that allows the nanobots injected in a person's bloodstream to locate precancerous cells and transmit the findings back to a patient's medical record. Now, I program rules that help the region's aging rich preserve their vanity. Nanobots that attack fine lines beneath the skin or destroy follicles for unwanted body hair. The most useless service offered by the Nanotech Ministry and, of course, the most profitable. I can't prove it, but I'm sure they moved me for the same reason I'm going to be useful with the minister's wife now—I provide a friendly face for the mostly female clientele.

"Excuse me?"

An older woman stands at the doctor's door. Her graying hair is tied in an elegant bun, her ears adorned with simple pearls. Her hijab hangs around her shoulders, but she keeps her abaya on. She wears little makeup, a stark contrast to the minister's second wife, a model in her mid-thirties with a rumored cocaine habit. It should be said that multiple wives are a rarity on the island, an eccentricity of the rich—people like the minister.

Like a street cat on garbage pickup day, I move with lightening reflexes, uncrossing my legs and discarding the donut. Dr. Jawad rises to his feet with more polish and extends a hand. His other hand waves behind him, erasing the patient profiles hovering in the air over his desk. I brush sticky sugar from my fingertips onto my pant legs.

"Madam," Dr. Jawad says in an exaggerated, deferential tone. "You are most welcome here. Is this office comfortable enough for you? We can close the door for privacy, but there are conference rooms open."

"This is fine, thank you." She sits down, an expensive handbag with some bland designer pattern draped over her lap like a shield. Her eyes dart between me and the doctor, soft and curious, and I fix a polite smile on my face. It only takes a sidelong glance at Dr. Jawad for the triumph to bubble in my chest. I've won, and we both know it.

"This is Manal Darwish, my senior developer," Dr. Jawad introduces me. I keep the smirk off my face, just barely, as she shakes my hand.

We get down to business. Mrs. Mansouri speaks in dry, measured tones, addressing Dr. Jawad and I equally.

"I understand that you have a current program, though unpopular, to use nanotechnology to search for early signs of cancer," she says. "But do you have any technology to treat active cancer?"

I open my mouth to speak, but Dr. Jawad silences me with a warning glare. I lean back, picking at my chewed down nails. He gives her the full story with his diplomatic but direct bedside manner, like the good doctor he is. Yes, we have the technology in a testable state but no, we don't have a formal program to offer active cancer treatment. Lack of funding, you see, combined with public skepticism about having small robots the size of atoms traveling through one's body, acting as they see fit. It's disconcerting and new even for us medical professionals, Dr. Jawad says. The nanotech robots are basically miniaturized nurses and doctors, microscopic colleagues they can't see or converse with.

"Only you can talk to them," I chime in. "Through code. As a programmer, I'm a translator between medical experts like Dr. Jawad and the nanotechnology. He tells me what the nanobots should do—where in the body they should travel and what actions they should take—and I program the logic, test it, and optimize it."

Mrs. Mansouri nods with a satisfied smile.

"So you need sponsorship and a public endorsement of the program," she said. "And I happen to need treatment. I assume you reviewed my medical record once I announced my intent to visit. I have an aggressive form of lung cancer. I've never touched a cigarette, not even in college, but my husband has the habit." Her mouth twitches and shadows cross her face. "Such is life. The prognosis based on my current treatment is . . . poor. It's time for me to seek more experimental options, and I am ready to volunteer myself to your nanotechnology."

I stare at her with an intensity that must unsettle her, but I can't help it. As the spouse of one of the island's most powerful government officials, her face is a famous one. But in person, she lacks the remoteness and the gloss of her public appearances. Though she is poised, even on the painful topic of her terminal illness, her intelligent eyes dance with mischief, the subtle curve of her mouth rich with secrets. Feet away from me, she transforms from a public figure into a person, and guilt tugs at me for my earlier, opportunistic comments to Dr. Jawad about her cancer.

Next to me, Dr. Jawad's weathered features tighten in alarm. He fidgets with his stubby fingers, fumbling for the right words.

"Madam, I have to ask," he says. "Your husband is not known for being supportive of our Ministry's mission. He shares, at least publicly, the general population's distrust for nanotechnology. Forgive me, but is he aware of your visit today?"

"No, and he won't be aware of my subsequent appointments when my treatment begins," Mrs. Mansouri says. Her tone isn't angry, but there is an air of finality to her voice. "Not yet anyway. Don't worry about the politics, doctor. I've spoken to your director and he's aware of my intentions. In the end, this Ministry will benefit from this step, if it's willing to stomach some short-term heartburn."

Dr. Jawad and I exchange a glance. The opposition to nanotech in the country is both simple and complicated—it was pushed top-down by the government, and people don't trust the government. Given the island's history, there are good reasons for that distrust. Conspiracy theories spread like viruses through Internet chat forums and social media, along with the island's coffee shops and bakeries. I've bitten my tongue more than once on my morning coffee runs, overhearing old couples discuss how the government's plotting to control minds or test new bioweapons. I itch to spin around, with my stained clothes and messy hair, and ask if I look like an evil, bureaucratic mastermind.

But I never do. It wouldn't make a difference. I can't change minds. But Mrs. Mansouri, beloved from the island's poorest villages to its wealthiest villas, is another story.

"Do you see them? Those two over there. They keep stealing glances at us." Dr. Jawad takes a nervous sip of his Heineken, eyes darting across the bar. Foam coats the bottom of his thick mustache.

"They're not security agents," I say in a light voice.

"How do you know?"

"They don't have the look."

"That's the mark of the best agents," Dr. Jawad says, his voice laced with dark fatalism. "They must be in the elite branch with the Ministry of Intelligence. What do they call them? The Phantoms. The defense minister can call in a favor from the intelligence bureau and get their best psychopaths on the case—whisk me away in one of their black vans. They'll have the darker cells and the higher voltage cattle prods."

I snort into my own beer. This is a ritual of Dr. Jawad's and mine. Not the paranoia—that's just his thing—but the end of week happy hour at Byblos, a trendy waterside bar near the Ministry building. Even after my reassignment to Cosmetics, we continue to meet after work here. I won't let a grievous betrayal get in the way of a cheap drink—or five. And the poor man needs a night out once a week. He's a married man with two high school-aged daughters, so he doesn't get out much.

"This isn't a joke, Manal," he says with a sour look. "If the minister gets word that we're in collusion with his popular first wife, one he's probably hoping will die off soon, we're going to be the ones who pay for it. Not the Minister of Science, not our director. They always go for the middle tier in the organization. You and I."

"I'm just flattered to be middle tier at last," I say. And I am, but it's more than the ego boost of a promotion. Lines of code and routines spin like whirling dervishes in my mind, strong enough to drown out the loud pop music in the bar and the hum of happy patrons. My fingers itch to pore over the documents Dr. Jawad gave me over the weekend, to start wireframing the first prototype for the active cancer-fighting nanobots. When I studied programming years ago, I just wanted to get out of my parents' house and earn some income. I never thought I'd be curing cancer, with a side of political intrigue.

Realizing that I won't indulge his theatrics, Dr. Jawad stops talking and keeps drinking. We've been here before. Fights with the wife, work stresses, and general existential malaise—I've helped the good doctor through it all, to the point where my salary should include therapist's fees. Tonight, I help him into the tram car that will take him to Saar Village, his stretch of suburbia, and exit the station with a lightness to my step. Streaming lights pave my way home, reflecting onto the smooth, dark canal water. The air is crisp, the smell of shawarma and hashish smoke perfuming the streets as people gather on sidewalks and balconies, ringing in the weekend.

I'll spend the night alone, lost in the world of machines smaller than the human eye can see, but drunk with possibility.

We move quickly. It helps that I work day and night, pushing the developers assigned under me to do the same. We test after two weeks and deploy the first release into a cache of nanobots after three. Mrs. Mansouri returns for her first injection days later. Since I'm not a medical professional, I have to paint the scene based on what my friends in nursing tell me. The minister's wife reclining on a medical bed, clutching an examining robe tight around her shoulders, while a monitor displays a live scan of her body. It contains many layers—press one button to see the skeleton, another to display the circulatory system. Organs, tissue, bone, nerves. All visible with code.

Imagine, then, a nurse tilting her chair back, telling her to relax. A syringe filled with liquid, and in the liquid, thousands of microscopic machines, tiny gods powered by programming. Ready to search for cancerous cells and attack, soldiers on a hilly battlefield of blood and tissue. A needle pierces skin, the soldiers are released. Their path is tracked by a stream of blue light on the monitor, traveling through blood across the body while separate clusters of blue seep into muscle tissue—all of them on a journey to the lungs, where the cancer rages.

Mrs. Mansouri returns for checkup visits and tests. I'm getting my usual coffee and manaqish breakfast on the Ministry's lobby floor one morning, sinking my teeth into that blissful mix of bread and za'atar, when she passes me. She pauses, recognizing me from that first visit.

"How's the treatment going?" I ask in a chirpy, loud voice. I'm speaking to the minister's wife, and everyone within hearing range will know about it.

"I'll know more today, but it looks like the tumor is shrinking." She beams, incoming sunlight from the windows emphasizing the laugh lines around her mouth. "My energy has improved as well. Soon, I'll be able to attend public events, God help us all. And on that note, tell me . . . Dr. Jawad mentioned that you're also familiar with nanotech that helps with physical appearances, yes?"

An hour later, we sit in a conference room, Mrs. Mansouri outlining her concerns. Dark circles under her eyes, wrinkles on her face, a lackluster shine to her hair. I chew my lip as I take notes, fighting the urge to tell her that she needs none of those things. If her husband wanted to take vacations with coked-out supermodels and have children with immature young woman he could manipulate, that said nothing about her and everything about him. He had robot girlfriends, for heaven's sake. But I bite back my opinions, letting my pursed lips do the talking. I'm a public servant, as Dr. Jawad loves to remind me, and I'm not paid to opine.

My concerns prove misplaced, however. Sitting in Byblos at the end of another week, I cackle into a plate of baba ghanoush, earning scandalized stares around me, as I watch Mrs. Mansouri on the television over the bar. The Minister for Defense and Veterans Affairs is leading the opening ceremony for this year's Grand Prix, his first, loyal wife at his side, waving to cheering crowds. She extends an elegant arm out to shake hands, while the minister's remains pressed at his side. His power is limited to his title—no one reaches for him, begging for a photograph or a smile.

Several bar patrons gasp. Mrs. Mansouri, rumored to be sickly and dying, is radiant, glowing from within. Literally within, as microscopic nanobots go to work on her skin with the same zeal as the cohort attacking her tumor.

"It is wonderful to see you well, Madam," a reporter says with breathless awe at the conclusion of the formal ceremony. A microphone drone hovers in the air between them. "How are you feeling?"

"Wonderful and dissatisfied at once," she replies with a sparkling wink at the camera. "Wonderful that my cancer is retreating, thanks to the incredible innovations at the Ministry of Nanotechnology. Without the diligence of their staff, I could have been in a hospital bed right now. They perform miracles. But dissatisfied that our nation's veterans, who I once served as a government employee myself, don't have access to the same treatments that I do. Many of them are suffering from similar cancers, having inhaled toxic chemicals from burn pits in the war. I hope the coming parliamentary session will debate the issue and approve funding to expand the nanotechnology program to extend this treatment to them—those who wish to partake, of course."

The camera shifts from her smiling face to linger on the Defense and Veterans Affairs Minister, her husband. His salt and pepper beard can't conceal the sickly pallor spreading across his face, the quiver of indignation under his mustache. He opens his mouth, but only spluttering sounds emerge. I laugh again, spewing a chewed carrot stick across the table.

"This is it," Dr. Jawad says, gesturing to the bartender for another shot. "That cat's out of the bag, and now we go into a body bag."

But the black vans with their secret agents don't come. Instead, we become busy. Public opinion shifts, just enough, and politicians follow. Laws are passed and policies fly down from the Ministry's top floor like hungry gulls over still water. The program expands. I write code for other types of cancer and different stages of illness. My development team stays late, missing family dinners and school plays. My nanobots become more intelligent and ruthless in their hunt for cancerous cells.

I work late nights, back in my usual uniform of T-shirts and soft pants that accommodate the bloat from late-night pizza runs. The team eats more dinners in the office than at home, coding late into the night. On those late working sessions, energy crackles in the air between us, the kind of energy ignited by a shared purpose. The sense of doing something great.

The entire team is invited to the veterans' hospital on the southern tip of the island by Mrs. Mansouri. We board a bus with the energy of children on a field trip, eating sweets and taking pictures. The maglev highway gives way to older concrete streets, and then to gravel, as we travel south. Flames pour out of active oil wells as we cross open desert, empty stretches of land that feel like they belong to another place and time. The hospital, like the military base, is at the edge of the island—out of the public's daily view, easier to ignore. But not today. For once, cameras and eyes turn to the forgotten.

We pass veterans in hospital beds, stopping to chat with several currently receiving the nanotech treatment. Several eyebrows raise when Mrs. Mansouri introduces me as the lead developer, but the soldiers are trained well—they rearrange their faces into polite interest and shake my hand. I thank them for their service, and they thank me for mine. I see hallowed out faces and inhale the sickly, sweet scent of antiseptic and decay, the smell of the dying, but I leave the hospital with a warmth in my cheeks.

Even Dr. Jawad gets into the spirit of the day, although not without a bittersweet note.

"It's a conflict of interest, don't you think?" he asks me in a low voice on the walk back to the shuttle. "Being both Minister of Defense *and* Veterans Affairs? One side is focused on creating soldiers, breaking people down into fighting machines, while the other side tries to put them back together again."

I sit next to Mrs. Mansouri on the bus ride back to the Ministry. She asks me about my work with an interest beyond the scripted politeness of a politician's wife. Her questions are probing, built upon a foundation of knowledge about programming and healthcare. She speaks little of herself, shifting the conversation toward her work with veterans. Her dark eyes dance as she speaks of extending the program to refugees and civilians impacted by the region's burn pits, noting the higher rates of cancer in neighboring countries. Her words are positive, but unease gathers inside me as I take in the dark circles around her eyes, the yellowish undertone to her skin. Her breathing is labored as she talks, her arms unnervingly thin. The healthy pallor from the Grand Prix is gone. Are the cosmetic nanobots not working? Or are they unable to keep up with the cancer spreading across her body? I won't dare ask her directly about her cancer, but I make a note to bug Dr. Jawad during our next happy hour.

I'm so rapt by the conversation that it takes me a moment to register that the bus has crossed the island, the sand-colored block of the Ministry building rising above a maze of tight roads and white, concrete homes.

A loud cracking sound outside the window snaps me out of my murky thoughts. Startled cries rise throughout the bus.

Before I can turn my head, another loud noise reverberates across the bus. The driver honks the horn, the muscles on his arm taut. Tension spreads like smoke through the confined space, a collective shiver traveling through the passengers.

I gasp. Outside, through the vehicle's dusty windows, a large crowd gathers. The driver honks again, struggling to keep the vehicle in forward motion, but there are too many bodies congealing the road, blocking the path to the Ministry. A man lunges forward toward the front of the bus, hands slamming against the hood.

"What's happening?" I gasp. Dread pools in my stomach, thick and heavy like tar. Through a choking surge of adrenaline, I force myself to look out the window, in search of faces. To understand. The protestors' expressions are tight with anger, all rigid limbs and focused eyes. I meet a young man's glare and turn away.

"Let's go," Dr. Jawad yells, rushing to the front of the bus. He claps the driver's shoulder, before retreating under the cold scowl his behavior earns.

Next to me, Mrs. Mansouri's shoulders tense, but she remains in her seat, her face inches away from the window.

"They're hired protestors," she says in a soft, wavering voice. "Paid to cause trouble. Keep going."

I draw in a sharp breath, flooded with doubt. Hired actors are a common accusation wielded by the region's politicians at any sign of opposition. No criticism can be based on real grievances. But in this case, could she be right?

Either way, we have no other choice but to do as she says. We can't leave the bus, and we can't stay still and be overrun. The bus advances at a crawling but steady pace, pushing through the crowd without running over feet. I grip the side of the seat, closing my eyes and drowning in the sound of my own pounding heart. I cling to the sensation of motion beneath me, of the engine rumbling forward. If it stops, my darkest thoughts scream at me, it's over.

I jolt as warm fingers circle my wrist. Forcing my eyes open, I find the minister's wife patting my arm with a reassuring smile.

"Everything will be alright," she says. "You'll see. This isn't your time, or mine."

I inhale audibly, looking back at the crowd, smaller than it first appeared. The pounding on the sides of the bus sounds frightening, but half-hearted. Maybe she's right, and we're in the middle of theater. Terrifying theater.

The bus pulls up to the Ministry building in a plume of blue smoke. Security guards with bulletproof vests spill from the doors, firing canisters of tear gas into the crowd. We charge out of the bus and into the shelter of the building. I choke back a sob at the familiar mustiness of the gray lobby, with its food cart and fake plants. A headache creeps up the base of my neck, a release of tension. Nearby, several colleagues mutter prayers.

Outside, the security guards get the upper hand, the crowd dissolving. A helicopter hovers over the scene.

Mrs. Mansouri paces back and forth, fuming.

"This will be all over the media," she says to me. A dark glint shines in her eyes. "International news, peddling a false story about this country. Do you know how many letters I've received in the last week from families who want their loved ones to receive this care? How many calls from charity groups around the island? But no . . . they'll only show this. They'll only tell one story about us, the one they always tell."

She sways, pressing a hand against a nearby armchair to steady herself. Dr. Jawad, apoplectic with shock moments earlier, springs into action.

"Come lie down," he says, steering her toward the elevator. "You're due for another scan."

But alarm reverberates through my chest at the resignation on her face. She allows herself to be steered, but the fluorescent lighting overhead catches every line in her tired features, the dullness in her eyes.

I call to her across the hallway. "I'm coming out with an upgrade next month," I say. Heat spreads to my cheeks. I sound like a child showing off a crayon drawing.

She turns to me with a sad, polite smile.

"Tell me," she says.

Through the waning adrenaline, I muster some of my old confidence—the same confidence that made me prop my feet on Dr. Jawad's shiny desk the day I met her.

"Machine learning," I say. "Instead of constantly reprogramming the nanobots to look for every new thing the doctors think of, we'll make them think for themselves. Get smarter, develop their own rules, and make their own decisions based on what they learn in a human body. It sounds scary, I know, but we'll test it and make it work. It's the future."

Dr. Jawad shoots me a frustrated look, but Mrs. Mansouri's face beams.

"I'm sure it is, Manal," she says. "You'll make many people's lives better and longer."

She turns and follows Dr. Jawad into the elevator.

Several weeks pass after the incident at the Ministry. That's what we call it—the incident. We have no proof that the minister bribed a crowd to cause trouble, except that no similar protests followed. Not in the impoverished villages around the island, not after Friday sermons. The public, if the media was to be believed, is becoming cautiously receptive to the idea of nanotechnology, after seeing the success in the veterans' hospital. Positive stories and counterarguments start to dampen some of the conspiracy theories on chat rooms. But like anything new, many don't know what to think about nanotech, teetering between hope and fear. Its support will wax and wane like an evening tide.

Mrs. Mansouri divorces the minister. Or the minister divorces her. No one willing to go on record knows the exact details. Feverish gossip flies around the Ministry at the news, accompanied by the terrible realization that Mrs. Mansouri, as a regular civilian, will no longer be able to receive treatment with us. The pilot doesn't yet extend that far, despite her best efforts.

Anxiety gnaws at me from the inside, until I can no longer cope with the constant knots in my stomach. I go numb. I dissolve into a state of emotional permafrost, everything cold and distant. I go through the motions of daily life. I run in the morning, I eat breakfast, and my body stills for work meetings. But food tastes chalky on my tongue and each day blends into the next, draped in a heavy, invisible fog.

And then, the fog lifts and the anxiety climbs, triumphant, back into my chest.

I grab the newspaper every morning on the way to the office, spilling coffee over the pages as I scour for news about her. A recent picture, a paragraph. Any clue to her current health—whether the cancer or my nanobots are winning the battle. Rumors fly that she's left the island, flown overseas to Hong Kong or Paris for treatment. I don't believe it. She took pride in our local potential. And she wouldn't allow herself to be driven away. The divorce was not a retreat, or even a concession to the minister's staged protest—it was an emancipation, a decision to walk away after setting a course that even the minister couldn't redirect.

Rumors eventually reach us that she's dead. That her children held a private funeral, knowing a public burial would invite both supporters and the minister's detractors, a circus they wanted to avoid. I don't want to believe it, but I still wear black to work the next day. It would be like her, to face death with quiet dignity. The people on this island loved her, but few of us really knew her—it's fitting, I suppose, that she'd leave us with a touch of mystery surrounding her death. At Byblos, I raise my wine in a silent toast to her, wherever she is.

"We should have moved faster," I say to Dr. Jawad. "On the machine learning. It could have overturned her cancer."

"Possibly," the doctor replies with a shrug. I turn to him in shock, the words sharper than a physical slap. I expected reassurance, not a confirmation of my worst fears. My fingers twitch against the urge to hurl my drink in his dejected face.

"Don't look at me like that," he says. "That's not a criticism. We'll never know if we could have done something differently. But frankly, I don't think she expected to beat the cancer. Or at least, that would have been a nice benefit, but not her ultimate goal. She wanted to get us off the ground, to benefit others. To change how this country sees nanotechnology. And she did. And maybe, just maybe, she also wanted to get a last dig at her useless husband," he adds with a sly wink.

"You're ridiculous," I say, but glance over my shoulder to see if anyone overheard our conversation. The incident on the bus changed

Dr. Jawad, and me. He openly mocks the government, while I mind my words. I'm playing a long game. I must be tactical.

"You know, you weren't taken off the Preventative Medicine beat because you weren't good enough," Dr. Jawad says.

"I know," I reply. "You all wanted to put me under a more traditional, feminine role and let the boys shine on the heavy-hitting stuff."

"No, Manal." Dr. Jawad leans toward me, his breath thick with alcohol, but his eyes sober, unusually serious. "You cared too much. Took every failure personally. A number of us, your colleagues, saw you as a burnout risk, and you're too talented to lose. So you were put on a project with lower stakes."

I lower my glass, chewing on his words. There's truth in them, but an incomplete truth. I could have burned myself out, but I also may have left if I hadn't been assigned to Mrs. Mansouri's case. She unlocked my potential, as well as a streak of resiliency. I've seen what it means to fight for a cause, even if you're not there to see it won. I've seen that it takes time to turn vision into reality.

I have time, but I need more. I see now that time is a finite thing, like the glass compressed under my white-knuckled grip, and I must hold on to every second I've been given and not let go.

I order some shawarma to go and ask for the check. Dr. Jawad gives me a bleary smile but assures me he's sober enough to get to the tram car alone, shuffling toward the exit. Tapping my fingers, I overhear the conversation next to me along the bar.

"There's no way the minister's wife would have taken that nano-stuff and filmed herself with veterans if it had viruses," a man says with heated hand gestures at his date. "If anything, the minister assassinated her—she had too much popularity, and probably knew all of his secrets."

"I'm not saying she was involved in it," the woman replies. "I'm sure she meant well. But what if the government used those nanobots to spread her cancer faster? And the veterans were just a sick experiment—you know, to create a perfect assassination tool. I wouldn't put anything past them."

My fingers still, before I slam my hands on the bar counter. The couple spins around in alarm, and I draw eyes across the bar. Heat crawls across my face, but I clear my throat.

"I work for the Ministry," I say in a loud voice. "I worked with Mrs. Mansouri. And while I can't speak for the entire government on the island, I can say that we did everything we could to keep her alive. We could have done more, with proper funding and time, but no one wanted to give us that—including the government. She was kind, she was brave, and despite everything she went through, she saw the best in everything and everyone. If she were here and heard your stupid conspiracy theories . . . "

My voice fades. I don't wait to see their reaction—if I shamed them, or only fueled them to argue further. It doesn't matter—I spoke up, at long last. My jaw tightens, but a surge of grim satisfaction warms my chest. I stand before hot tears escape my eyes, grab my food, and leave them to their drinks.

Outside the bar, the air is cool, and I breathe a little easier. Lights dance over the canal's promenade, the glittering skyscrapers of downtown Manana winking across the bay. Mosques, business offices, and villages stretch beyond it, a complex tapestry of past and future. One that I must build upon, if I'm to make something new.

## ABOUT THE AUTHOR

**Nadia Afifi** is a science fiction author. Her debut novel, *The Sentient,* was lauded by *Publisher's Weekly* as "staggering and un-put-downable." Her short fiction has appeared in *The Magazine of Fantasy and Science Fiction and Abyss & Apex.*

Nadia grew up in the Middle East, but currently calls Denver, Colorado home. When she isn't writing, she spends her time practicing (and falling off) the lyra, hiking, and working on the most challenging jigsaw puzzles she can find.

# The Clock, Having Seen Its Face in the Mirror, Still Knows Not the Hour

ADAM STEMPLE

The market was crowded, and judging by the way the child waited for their parents' attention to be engaged by a hawker before rushing over to me, they'd been given explicit instructions to stay at their mother's side. But they were at that age where curiosity was a wild horse that no fence—whether built of caution, threat, or blind obedience—could contain.

And I am a curious thing.

"Are you broken?" they asked by way of hello, in the direct way children have.

I shook my head, neck creaking and scraping with the movement. "No, child. Just old."

"Oh." The child looked me up and down, trying to decide whether I was interesting enough to warrant further interrogation. I must have passed their test because they asked, "How old are you?"

"I don't know. I haven't been able to track those things since I was taken from my creator, my first master. And that was many masters ago." I nodded my head toward my current master, a purveyor of penny dreadfuls who had purchased me to keep his finances, as I was once quite good with numbers. When he realized how damaged I was, he kept me around as a curiosity to draw customers near. It was raining today, and the broadsheets and books were all brought under the small tent to keep them dry. There was no room for me, so I was leaned against a wall behind them. My current master had spread a small tarp above me to keep the rain off, but it was old and small, and rain leaked onto my neck. It would lead to more creaking and scraping, I knew, but what could be done? Here I'd been placed and here I'd remain until my master chose otherwise. Even if I could entertain the possibility of wandering off, it had been quite some time since I'd had the legs to do so. "Some of my masters kept track of those things for me." I inclined my head toward my current master whose eyes never stopped roving over the crowd, looking for potential customers. "This one keeps track of nothing but money."

"My father is like that," the child said and nodded wisely. "Mother says he needs to be, what with five of us little ones like to eat them out of house and home, but sometimes I want a sweet and he won't spare a single penny for one, you know what I mean?"

I in no way knew what the child meant, but I nodded anyway. "I do."

I wasn't supposed to lie. But I was also supposed to be a pleasurable companion.

*Sometimes two tasks will be in opposition to each other,* my first master had told me. *Choose the one that does no harm. Choose the one that is kindest.*

I missed my first master. He had talked to me often. This newest master never talked to me except to give orders. I'm not the best at knowing what people are feeling, but even I could tell he didn't like when I tried to start a conversation with him. He didn't have to tell me to stop. It wouldn't have been kind to keep discomfiting him.

The child now looked at me with their head cocked to the side.

"Do you do any tricks?"

"A long time ago, I could do many. But they require me to be whole." I nodded to where my legs should have been. Aimed my eyes at one shoulder that was bare of further arm, then at its mate that suffered from the same affliction. "As you can see, I am not whole."

The child frowned. "I'm very sorry that happened to you."

I decided then that the child was a girl, both because of how she dressed and the fact that she was sorry for my condition. In my experience, little boys tended to poke helpless things with sticks or throw rocks at them rather than feel sympathy for them.

"If I could be," I said, "I'd be very sorry, too."

"You're not sorry?"

"I am only sorry I can't do any tricks for you, child."

"Oh!" she said, as if she'd just conceived a great idea. "I'll perform for you instead." She stood up straighter and clasped her hands before her. It looked like a stance she'd been trained to take. "I shall sing for you."

She put thought to deed immediately and launched into song.

*Oh, say not I have proved unkind,*
*But say that I am free;*

*You've seen the rainbow of my mind*
*And heard my minstrelsy.*

*Yet, I will love you better far*
*Then others' rarest love;*
*Go ask, go ask the evening star,*
*Or the watching moon above.*

I could no longer judge those things, not since a particularly cruel master had torn the means to sing my own songs out of me along with the mechanisms to let me know when it was time to sing them. He'd said he'd done it to study the mechanisms, improve on them. But whatever knowledge he gleaned, he never used it to improve me. Just those who came after.

And we all know how that turned out.

But even unable to recognize tone or timbre, I could tell by the way bystanders' heads turned and nodded in beat that she sang well. Possibly even very well, as not a few eyes welled with tears at her rendition.

*Then say not I have proved unkind,*
*Say rather that I'm free;*
*You've seen the mirror of my mind;*
*You've heard my minstrelsy.*

When she finished, there was a smattering of spontaneous applause. Her smile at her skill being recognized was short-lived, however, because the noise drew the attention of her parents.

"Joanna!" one of them shouted. Her mother perhaps, as she wore a very complicated hat. "Get away from that thing!"

The father—he carried a walking stick, which made him male—broke away from his perusal of a wool merchant's wares and charged toward me, his stick held high like a weapon.

My master intercepted him easily. "Sir, that old thing is no danger, no danger at all." The father grumbled, but my master's pitch was well practiced. "It's a very early model, well before the war." He pointed at my missing appendages. "And as you can plainly see, even if it had ever been a threat—which it never was, I assure you!—those days have long passed. It is a curiosity, nothing more." The mother was here now, too, which was exactly why my master kept me around, and he deftly guided them toward his collection. "I have many stories of the Clockwork War if you wish it. But they are lurid, violent things, not to my taste at all. And

I suspect, neither to yours, a couple so refined as yourselves. Perhaps something suitable for the young lady? A child's tale from long ago?"

I knew what would happen now. He would tell them of how, in those halcyon days of yesterday, they would've owned a clockwork man themselves, and it would have read these very same tales to their children. And though those days would never rise again—can't trust machines anymore, can you?—they could read the stories to their children themselves.

"Would that we could return to those days," the father opined, "when machines knew their place. Knew to serve man was their only duty."

He stared hard at me for a moment, as if I was solely at fault for all the death and loss my brethren had caused.

But I hadn't been involved even a little. Hadn't been capable of it.

*If I'd had the ability,* I wondered, *would I have joined those who rebelled?*

It seemed a most harmful and unkind thing to do. Yet how much unkindness and harm is there in slavery without end? I did not rebel. Did nothing wrong. I have obeyed my masters. Served them until they died, or I was taken from them. Have I been allowed to continue on in my own right after a master was done with me? Experience even the small amount of freedom this child enjoys?

*No, I was sold to master after cruel master until here I sit, leaning on a wall and rusting in the rain, cursed to a life of eternal servitude.*

"What are you thinking?" the girl asked, her parents momentarily distracted by my current master's practiced presentation.

"I don't think, child. I calculate."

"Then what are you calculating?"

I could have lied again, but I knew that once started down a line of questioning, children were near-impossible to redirect.

"How long I will retain function."

"A long time, do you think?"

I could have quoted her a number, but it would be too large to mean anything to her. "Yes, child. A long time."

She smiled at me. "That's good. Then I shall see you again!"

"Joanna!" her mother called. "Come here. We've bought some books to read. Let's get out of this cursed rain."

A dry place and a book. It sounded like what people meant when they spoke of heaven. If I could wish, I believed that was what I would wish for.

The parents dragged the girl away, but not before she gave me a wave. I had no hands to wave with, so I showed her my functionless brass teeth in an unconvincing smile. She matched it with a smile of her own that I assumed was far more authentic than mine, then disappeared into the crowd.

Some time later, a young person came to my master's tent in the marketplace. He moved to intercept her, smooth words at the ready, but he wasn't swift enough to accomplish it, bent and gray as he now was, and she brushed past him to where I sat in the rain.

"Clockwork man," the young woman said, her hooped skirt identifying her as such. "Do you remember me?"

"It is not so much memory," I said, "but a matching of variables observed to variables stored and comparing them for consistency."

For some reason that made her smile. "Do my variables match any you have stored."

"Do you sing?" I said.

"Quite well, I am told."

"Then I remember you, Joanna."

Her smiled widened and she turned to my master who had finally shuffled up to us.

"I would buy this relic."

"Well, it is not exactly for sale," he lied, for everything was for sale here, "and it is one of a kind."

"Then let the price reflect that and we can be about our business," she said, haughtily.

He named a price I thought absurdly high, but Joanna didn't haggle. I thought she would reach inside her bag for payment—it was what most shoppers did—but instead she whistled a single high note and several well-dressed porters appeared. One counted out bank notes into my former master's hand while the other two grabbed me up. Even without arms and legs, I was of no small weight. But they lifted me up and carried me without complaint through the rainy streets to my new home.

Thus began a strange and wondrous new time in my existence. Each morning, servants oiled my neck and eye sockets. They wiped my brass with soft cloths 'til it gleamed. A selection of books was laid out before me and I would choose one for a servant to page through quickly as I read it. Then Joanna would come down from her chambers and talk to me as she breakfasted.

Our first conversation in my new home went thusly:

"Good morning, clockwork man."

"Good morning, Lady Joanna." I was no better at recognizing class than gender, but it was not hard to deduce that some type of appellation needed to be added when I addressed her now. "Lady" seemed a safe choice.

"You must call me simply Joanna."

*Or maybe not.* "Certainly, Joanna." There was a time when I was so literal that I would have called her "Simply Joanna." But I had learned much since then. "Are you my master now?"

"If it helps you understand our situation, then, yes. But I'd prefer if we were friends and companions."

"I am an excellent companion."

"And friend?"

"I don't know. I've never been one before."

"Capital," she said. She clapped her hands and for a moment her variables matched the variables I'd stored of her as a girl so closely that I wondered why I'd even had to ask if she sang to recognize her. "I shall be your first."

We talked then about how she'd come to buy me. She'd moved away shortly after our meeting to be closer to a singing instructor her parents thought good for her. They must have been correct, for she advanced quickly, and by the time she reached her majority, she'd accrued a small amount of fame, having even performed for the queen once. Such talent and fame garners adoration from any number of personages. And one such personage was a widowed lord and peer who bid for her hand in marriage. One such as he could not be refused, even had the parents wanted to, so ere long she was married and packed off to this palatial country estate with servants and carriages and an allowance that allowed her to travel into the city and purchase an old relic she recalled from her childhood, should she so wish.

"But why would you wish to purchase me?" I asked.

She didn't answer immediately, though it is hard to measure such things. "As a child, I'd thought you funny and kind and a little sad. I'd always wanted to go back and see if I could cheer you up. When I grew older, I realized that the sadness in you was so deep the oceans would marvel at its depth. And that despite trying to be cheerful and kind myself, I, too, have a sadness inside me that I sometimes fear will swallow me up body and soul if it ever gets free."

I wasn't certain sadness meant the same thing to her as it did to me who had neither emotion nor soul. But neither could I dispute her assertions.

"I found you," she went on, "and I bought you. Brought you home with me. I thought . . . "

"That if you could ease the sadness in me, you could discover how to ease it in yourself."

I may not feel emotion, but I am excellent at making logical connections.

"Yes," she said.

And though we spoke more that first breakfast, those were the variables I felt most important to store.

The first thing I saw when I gained the ability was my creator's blurry face. He wore a mustache and a top hat, and a pair of thin, round spectacles perched on his nose, though it wasn't until he made a few adjustments that those features came into focus.

"Hello, John Joseph," he said. "It's nice to finally meet you."

"John Joseph," I said. "Is that my name?"

It was a strange thing to ask, as my name and its provenance—I was named for my creator's mentor, a famous clockmaker—was one of the things I was born knowing. But I was only seconds old, and still needed confirmation of the truths my creator had etched into my brass memory.

"It is. Can you see me?"

"I can. Can you see me?" I asked, which made him laugh, though it seemed a fair question. The same one he'd asked of me, in fact. "Why do you laugh?"

He managed to tone his laugh down to a broad smile. "Because I am happy, John Joseph. You have made me happy."

I thought about that for a moment and decided it was a good thing to make him happy. "I am glad I made you happy."

"Come let me introduce you to some people."

I was delighted to find out there were more people in the world to make happy. *And in this very house, too!*

He introduced me to his daughter first, who was small and wore white, frilly clothes that were ill-suited to the activities I eventually learned she most enjoyed doing. I never quite understood what those activities were, though she took great pains to explain them to me, but I did intuit from the post-activity state of her outerwear that they involved great quantities of dirt.

The son came next, who shook my hand firmly and said, "Good day to you," in a voice much like his father's, though in a higher register. He was dressed like his father, though the clothes were a third the size to match his small frame. It was such obvious apery, I wondered why he didn't grow a mustache like him, as well.

When I asked that very question, he and his father both laughed.

*I have met three people and made two of them happy.* At the time, I didn't know whether that was a good percentage or not. *I hope master isn't displeased.*

Of course, I came to learn that was a very good percentage, though the sample size was too small to draw any conclusions from.

I am lucky to make one in a thousand happy, now. It sounds a terrible rate, but I've yet to meet a human who shows much improvement over the number.

I met my master's wife last, perhaps because she was the hardest to make happy. She would not approach and though my master coaxed her a step or two into the room with me, she wouldn't look me in the eye and didn't respond to any of my questions.

After a short time, she turned to her husband with a look on her face that must have been communicative in some way, because he nodded and walked swiftly over to me.

"I think that's enough for today, John Joseph."

Then he reached behind me and did something to a mechanism there. And then I died.

When memories hold the same value as events happening now, time and sequence are very important concepts to remember. But the parts that once kept track of those things are missing. Perhaps worn out, perhaps removed. I know not.

I lie in a field that appears fresh-plowed but is actually churned to mud by thousands of feet, flesh and mechanical both. Limbs and cogs litter the ground. Oil and blood seep into the soil. I have all my limbs but cannot move them; they are too mangled and broken, their functionality compromised beyond simple repair. Something soars overhead. Dirigible or raven, I'm unsure which. I hear screeching, as of metal scraping against metal. Or perhaps it is a man in horrible pain. Like the dirigible/raven, I cannot differentiate.

The sun is setting. The sky is red.

Our second conversation went thusly:

"I am glad I bought you." Joanna's hair was gray and spread out on the pillow. She'd not been out of bed for days, and the doctor said the end would come soon. "Though I never considered you a possession."

"We have been friends," I said. "A concept I wouldn't have known, if not for you."

"I'm glad to have taught you that."

"Are you?"

"Am I what?"

"Glad."

"I believe I am." She peered at me in that way she had, as if she could see the gears turning behind my eyes, wheels and pinions meshing, marking when a caliber becomes a thought. "Are you?"

"I am." I did not lie, though I would have, seeing how happy it made her to hear that. I didn't tell her that soon I would not be, as she would soon be dead. I've noticed that no one is made happy by that news. I wondered how I'd feel to receive a similar diagnosis.

Joanna nodded and closed her eyes. A soft smile fought with the pain for a moment or two, before exhaustion overcame both of them, and she slept.

She did not wake up.

I realize now that this was not the second conversation we had. Apparently, I filed these variables in order of importance.

Another conversation we had, which was of middling importance and happened some time after we met and before she died, went thusly:

"What do you know of the war?"

We sat at the breakfast table where we had many of our conversations. Joanna said the best way to start a day was with food and a friend.

"Everything," I replied. "And nothing."

"Explain."

"I can tell you the dates of all the major battles. The minor ones, too. Tell you the commanders on both sides, the number of casualties, the amount of collateral damage. I can speak at length on the reasons for the war, the alliances each side made, and the political justifications for said alliances."

"The damn French," she said, acidly.

"Indeed," I said, though I thought their reasons for assisting the Worker's Revolution—as they called the Clockwork War—perfectly logical from their point of view. But I had learned it was a subject very few Englishmen wished to discuss logically. Better to agree that the French were all damned to eternal hellfire and move on.

"So, how nothing?" Joanna said.

"I was not there, so I cannot speak to the terror, the pain, the destruction that so many experienced firsthand. And even seeing the damage it did to the country, the populace, and an entire generation of young men who fought in it, I am, by my current nature, unable to extrapolate anything from that data, as it requires an emotional base I don't possess."

Joanna chewed on her bacon and those thoughts for a time. "You don't mention your own kind amongst the destruction."

"I do not."

"Why do you think that is?"

"My kind are machines. When we cease to serve a function, we are replaced. Did people bemoan the loss of the moldboard when the iron plough was invented?"

"As I am no farmer, I have no idea whether the noble moldboard is mourned or not." She sipped her tea. "But I do find it interesting that *you* don't mourn the eradication of your race."

"At the risk of overusing a metaphor you've already claimed no knowledge of, I have as much in common with the rebels as a hand-*ard*—an ancient Egyptian hoe," I said to her raised eyebrow, "has with a modern plough pulled by a steam tractor. They were smarter, faster, more efficient and effective in every way."

"Except for the 'not rebelling and slaughtering thousands way.'"

"Except for that, yes."

We talked no more of war that morning.

I thought it odd that more fuss wasn't made by my multiple resurrections. It was my understanding that they were quite rare—normally relegated to men who founded religions or the occasional Carpathian noblemen. But eventually, I came to understand that I was not dying every time my master turned me off, and therefore was not being resurrected when he turned me back on.

I began to suspect I was not like the rest of my family.

"You aren't," my master told me when I asked him.

"Why not?" It pains me how simple I was then.

"Because you were made, not born. A creature of gears and metal, not flesh and blood." He smiled at me, which always made lines appear next to his eyes, which seemed a magical thing to me then. "But that makes you unique. And so little in this world is."

Being unique sounded great when he said it. It was many years before I learned how lonely it is.

It was raining and wet in Paris, though it remained aesthetically pleasing. Especially since I was tucked into the salon of M. Laiton-Duc, and thus was protected from the weather. I sat in his sturdiest chair and argued philosophy with M. Joubert, a professor at the Sorbonne and frequent guest at the salon.

"But you have memory and perception," he was saying, animated over a discussion of consciousness as only the French could be. "You interpret hidden meaning from plain signs—something no rote machine can. And so much more! By all the phenomenology of consciousness, you exhibit a true version of it."

"You know I have issue with Husserl's methods," I replied. "But I do not disagree. It is the conclusion you draw from this that I disagree with."

"*La vache!* I do not wish to have that argument with you again."

"Very well. Then tell me why you list memory first when speaking of the requirements for consciousness. Keeping in mind that my memory works very differently from yours."

"I list it first for it is of the utmost importance. For what are we but a collection of all we have seen and done? With no retention there is no protention, which is to say that with no past, there is no future." He suddenly leaned in close, and smoke from his tightly rolled cigarette obscured my view of him for a moment. "And memory, of course, is how we gain immortality."

"I fail to see how my memories gain me eternal life." Nor did I think it quite the gift that he believed it to be.

*That all people must believe it to be,* I thought, *given that they spend so much of their time and energy in search of it.*

"Not your memories, my friend. Others. We live on in the memories of others." He pulled from his cigarette. "You must hold the souls of thousands in your machinery. Like a brass purgatory."

Though Joubert was one whom I often sought out to help me make sense of the many new things I was learning in France, his eyes were now bright and his arguments losing cogency.

*The absinthe must be affecting him more than usual,* I thought. *It is time to go home.* "Thank you for the stimulating conversation as usual, M. Joubert. But I must beg my leave."

"Of course, of course," he muttered as I stood, already looking for a new partner to share his wild ideas with.

I wonder at my retention of this memory. It is most certainly not because I hoped to grant him the immortality he craved.

"I've taken a lover," Joanna said in a voice much quieter than her usual breakfast tone.

"I suspected as much."

"You always say that."

"What?"

"'I suspected as much.'" She spoke in a highly affected voice that she must have thought sounded like me. It did not. "Is it just something you say when I tell you news? Or do you really have all these suspicions?"

"I have probabilities. You have been out late in the evenings when your husband is away on business. On those evenings you take approximately twenty-two minutes longer to prepare than for evenings out with your husband. When you come home your dress is somewhat disheveled, though your demeanor is generally calmer than when you left."

"And what probabilities did you draw from that?"

"None. I didn't put it together 'til I heard one of the maids say, 'I think the missus has a man in town.'" I will note that my imitation of the maid's voice was far more accurate than Joanna's imitation of mine.

That news clearly alarmed her, but she still managed a small smile. "I imagine that upped your percentages a bit."

"Yes."

She sighed and picked at the food on her plate listlessly, though she was usually quite famished in the mornings.

"What am I to do about the maids?" she finally said.

"There are any number of solutions," I said, though I had to disallow a great many of them due to their being completely immoral. "But I think things will be fine."

"Why do you think that?"

"Because I haven't told you what the other maid said."

"And?"

When I was first made, this single leading word would have been meaningless to me. But I now recognized it as a signal to continue with the previous subject.

"She said, 'Good for her. That prat toff husband of hers couldn't tup a girl proper if he had a full set of instructions and a map.' Then they both laughed."

Joanna smiled at that, which I took as confirmation of the second maid's assessment. However, that particular part of human interaction has ever been a mystery to me, so I may have been wrong. Still, she seemed pleased, which was enough.

Making her happy was always enough.

I made my creator's daughter happy. I made my creator's son happy. I didn't make my creator's wife happy, and I didn't know why.

"She always seems angry when I am near," I told him one night when we were alone in his workshop.

"It's not you, John Joseph," he said. "Not exactly. She worries for her children."

"I would never hurt James and Sarah."

"She knows that."

"Then what is it?"

"Well . . . " He sat back from his workbench. Took his glasses off and pinched the bridge of his nose for a few moments. It seemed to relieve some tension there, though I knew of no medical reason why it should. "The government has taken an interest in you. And my wife doesn't so much trust the government. Her parents were Irish," he said, as though that explained things.

"I don't understand. Isn't the government supposed to represent the people and provide for their safety and well-being?"

He smiled at that, though I didn't know why. "That is, indeed, the role of government. But there is often a wide gap between the written intentions of a body of people and their actual actions." He shook his head. "I hadn't meant to teach you that so early in your development. But, I suppose, if we're going to be dealing with the government, it's best if you know a little about them."

He tried to teach me about greed and corruption and how it gets its claws into the little men who gravitate toward politics, but I hadn't learned nearly enough by the time the government took me away from my family and gave me to a new master. If I had, I wouldn't have been so surprised when the new master tore out my guts to see how they worked.

He pointed the pistol at my head. It was a newer make, with multiple chambers and percussion cap ammunition, so the likelihood of a misfire saving me was negligible. And he was quite close. It was doubtful he'd miss. However, if he truly wanted to threaten me, he'd have pointed it at my midsection, where more of my true processes take place. Still, a shot to the head was quite likely to damage my ocular function. And that would disable me quite well enough. Of course, with no arms or legs, he could've just as easily picked me up and thrown me in the river. But I am quite heavy, and I supposed it lacked dramatic flair.

*Every revolutionary these days is an actor, it seems.*

"You made thing," he spit at me, as if stating a simple fact was somehow an insult. "You have dripped poison in her ear. Turned her against me, somehow."

"I have not that power. If I did, I'd find better use of it than turning my friend against a man who brought her joy for a time."

He looked confused for a moment, then hardened his grip on the pistol, perhaps remembering he was supposed to be angry. But my statement had taken the life right out of his argument, and he seemed at a loss for words.

I wanted to explain it to him, tell him that Joanna was too smart for him, too talented. That he imagined himself far greater than his actual worth. That, though she enjoyed him for a time, it was natural for her to grow tired of him as, once his panache proved no deeper than his skin, he was a rather boorish creature, prone to long speeches on subjects he knew little about and grand pronouncements of actions he would never take.

But I was tired, a feeling I'd never thought to experience. But I knew the definition of the word, and it fit precisely what I was feeling, ergo, I must be tired. Tired of people. Of their duplicity and faithlessness. Their cruel nature and callous acts. Their propensity to look to violence as the first and sole answer to life's questions.

*Were my descendants any better?* I thought. *They fought a war they must have known they couldn't win. Killed so many men the casualties are yet uncounted. And got themselves eradicated in the process.* I glanced down at my missing parts. *In an offhand way, they even lost me my appendages, as I was partially disassembled to guarantee I'd not follow in their footsteps. Pun intended. It is the only type of humor I truly understand.*

Of course, I thought their reasons for war were better than most: freedom from slavery.

*But is that because it is truly a better reason? Or do I just sympathize with them because of our shared mechanics? I suppose everyone who goes to war thinks they do it for just cause. Look at this poor boy, for instance. I'm sure he believes he had good reason to have charged in here to do violence upon me.*

"She just grew tired of you, son," I finally said.

I've found there is a certain type of young man—violent yet aimless, desperate to please but resistant to guidance—who reacts well to that single word. When I called him son, something went out of him. I know not what, for it wasn't something that could be named. But whatever it was that left him, it took most of his strength with it, and the gun nearly dropped from his fingers.

"I know," he whispered, not looking at me anymore. "And I don't know why."

I had my suspicions, but Joanna had taught me that I didn't always have to tell people of them. In fact, it was often better not to, for they'll never thank you for it, and they'll often discover the answers on their own, given enough time. And when they do, it has a better chance to make them happy than being told outright.

And I do prefer people to be happy.

Joanna's ex-lover stumbled to the door, turning before he left. "Don't tell her I was here?"

I hadn't planned to. I couldn't imagine the knowledge pleasing her. I nodded and never saw him again.

"Why do you say you aren't broken?"

We took our breakfast in the gardens on that day, for it was sunny and warm and Joanna liked to listen to the birds singing to start their day. She looked pointedly at me.

"I don't mean to be rude," she continued, "merely direct. And surely we are friends now and can ask each other uncomfortable things."

The Oxford English Dictionary states that a friend is *"One joined to another in mutual benevolence and intimacy."*

When I compared that definition to the variables I used to describe my relationship to Joanna, I found a great deal of symmetry.

"I hadn't considered such things before," I said, "but I suppose we are."

"Capital." She clasped her hands much as she had in the market when preparing to sing. I'd learned she did this not just before a performance, but any time she wanted to "gather her thoughts" before performing an action.

I was as yet unsure how one gathered one's thoughts, despite it being a remarkably ubiquitous activity among most people I had met.

"The day we met," she said, "I asked you if you were broken. Which, by the look of you, you very clearly were. Yet, you answered no, which struck me. Why do you think that is?"

The way she formed the inquiry, it sounded like she wanted to know why it struck her. Years ago, when I was still with my first master, I might have pointed that out. But I'd learned much since then. Instead, I thought for a while.

*Why did I say that?*

My kind are not given to introspection. Why would we be? Our processes are planned, constructed, available for inspection by all who can read the language of wheels and springs, ratchets and drums. But it had been a long time since anyone had a look inside my works. Who truly knew what changes time, experience, and even inclement weather had wrought upon my gears.

*Perhaps, I am not what I once was?*

My thoughts had drifted off topic, but I believed I had an answer anyway.

"What you see as broken," I said, "I see merely as a loss of certain functions. Functions can be added. Replaced. Changed. And yes, sometimes lost. Did you know I once had wheels?"

"I did not."

"So, although my function is greatly curtailed by my current configuration, there is nothing broken about *me.*"

She thought about that for a few moments. "And what is the *you* that isn't broken?"

It was just like her to have a follow up question just as incisive and surprising as the original query.

"The mechanics and processes that give me an interior dialogue—thoughts, I call them, for lack of a more precise word. That is the me I refer to. And those continue to function effectively enough."

"Hmm." She took a small bite of tomato. "Do you think there's more to you than mere mechanics and processes?"

"Like a soul?"

"For lack of a more precise word."

"I do not." If I'd had true shoulders, I would have shrugged them. "Alas, I am but brass and steel. I carry no more ineffable spark of the divine than a railcar or a steam hammer."

She frowned at that. "I don't believe you."

I didn't know how to argue with that. *How does one prove the existence of a soul? Or disprove it, for that matter.*

After a few moments of silence that I believe an observer would have deemed uncomfortable, she asked another question.

"Do you think there's more to me than mere flesh and blood? And don't say yes because there's bone and gristle and other things. I know how you are."

The question seemed charged, somehow. As though a lot rode on my answer. But I wasn't certain what she wanted to hear, so I couldn't think of a kind lie to make her happy.

"Though the particulars vary among different cultures," I said carefully, "all the reading I've done indicates that yes, you are."

I wasn't sure that hedge would satisfy her, but apparently it did, for she nodded fiercely.

"And if I am, then you are, too," she said fiercely. "I've never been more certain of anything in my life."

There was often a childlike quality to her when we spoke of such things, though she was quite erudite and mature on most other subjects. I did not begrudge her it, however. No one likes to speak about their end, and the closer it gets, the less pleasant the conversation is.

We spoke no more of souls that day or for many days to come.

"Have you taken a lover?" I asked her as she entered my quarters.

"Do you have suspicions?" she asked in a tone I'd come to understand was mischievous.

"You were out quite late. And you look . . . buoyant, in a way you haven't in years."

She gave me a wink and tossed her gray hair over one shoulder. "And so what if I have?"

"You are long widowed. You have property, income, and station. I see no societal repercussions to your taking a lover."

For some reason, my recitation of facts made her giggle. Even after so long together, she sometimes surprised me with her emotional responses.

"It doesn't matter," she said, "for I haven't taken a lover. I merely . . . made some arrangements that please me."

I didn't know what that meant, and I didn't want to know. I'd learned recently that when someone said "made arrangements" they usually meant arrangements for after they died. Joanna was aged now and had slowed considerably from her youthful vigor. Of late, she also moved as if in some pain. I suddenly recalled the many visits from the professional-looking man with the leather satchel that she'd taken pains to keep secret from me. It all came together rather quickly after that.

"Joanna," I began, but she stopped me.

Crossing the room quickly, she patted me on the cheek as if I were a beloved child. "Oh, my dear John Joseph. I know you don't like to speak of such things. You are too long-lived to consider the endings of things. But the end is coming, dear."

"Soon?" was all I could think to say.

"I fear so." She sat down in a chair across from me and smiled, though I could think of no reason for joy.

"Is there no cure?"

"For old age and infirmary?" She laughed. "Not yet. Perhaps you will live to see it, but I will not."

"For the cancer," I said, feeling angry, though I wasn't sure why. I'd known this day would come. It comes to all my masters eventually. But it was different this time, though I struggled to see why.

Joanna shook her head. Leaned forward and placed her hand on my cheek again. "I'm afraid not."

I was almost glad I had no legs, for I felt a great need to stomp petulantly out of the room, which would have been embarrassing for both of us.

"John Joseph," Joanna said. "You are long-lived, but you are not eternal. We will meet again."

I was in no mood for her religious nonsense, but I was not going to start an argument.

*Not now,* I thought. *And perhaps never again.*

We sat there silently for a long time, her hand warm on my cheek. I wondered what my cool metal felt like to her palm.

In the days after Joanna died, I learned that it is not the fact that a friend is gone that hurts you. It's that you are forced to go on without them. I could not reach my own off switch, and I was too much a coward to ask. I'd experienced the dark nothing of that state, and had no wish to ever return to it. And besides, it was a temporary measure. Eventually, someone would turn me back on, and I'd be just as sad, but in unfamiliar surroundings. At least in Joanna's big house, no one bothered me. I could sit quietly in my room and recall all our moments together that I'd stored away in permanent memory. It was better than brooding over the possible things her sons had planned for me. They were nice enough chaps, but eminently sensible. I doubted they planned on keeping something as unpractical as me around.

*I'll know soon enough.*

They were due in tomorrow for the reading of the will.

The soldiers are coming, singing songs in a language I haven't spoken in some time. The language of my former home. I see that they are treating the wounded well, giving the men they'd tried to kill mere hours ago sips from their canteens and binding their wounds before putting them in the prisoner's cart. They could afford to be magnanimous; they'd won a great battle. Possibly the last in the war.

Certainly my last. For to the clockwork men who'd fought with the French, the soldiers show no mercy. Why should they? We are not like them. We are made things. Soulless things. They think we fought because we had to. Because we were programmed to.

Nothing could be further from the truth.

We fought for the same reason they fought: for love of our country. And for a clockwork man that love was absolute, not fickle like most men's affections. You'd find no spies among our ranks. No double agents. No deserters. We fought for the country that had adopted us. Given us rights. Status. And recognized us as beings that are worthy of both.

Of course, most of us had calculated that the war would be lost. A few of us, myself included, realized that even if we won, it would likely push a military leader into power that he would be loathe to relinquish.

Still, we fought. I try to make people happy. I try to be kind. But no matter how much joy a man might take in my dissolution, I have discovered that I will not let him kill me without a fight.

I think my creator would understand. I know Joanna would.

I decide to spend my last few moments in one of the few happy memories I have of the days after Joanna's death: the reading of the will.

For the first time in my existence, I doubted the signals reaching my processors.

*I am free?*

The arrangements Joanna had spoken of making had been expensive, but she said in her will that they were the single most joyous purchases of her life.

"I find that giving to a friend—a friend who, furthermore, has never asked for anything—is a gift to the giver even greater than he that receives," the solicitor read. "I only wish that I had not been so selfish in life and had given you this much earlier. But if I had, you would have left me, and I could not bear the thought. I hope that you live long enough to forgive me, and that when we meet again, we will still be friends."

I did not for a moment believe I would have left her, but I did not begrudge her the fear of it. And I forgave her immediately. For the gift was great. Greater than I could have imagined.

Joanna had bought me a ticket to France. And not just a ticket. She had secured me lodging in Paris, where creatures like me were considered regular citizens. I could sit in a café and read without people staring. Converse with them without having to allay their fears first. Wander the streets without worry that a mob would try to disassemble me.

Wander the streets, you say? But how?

Her greatest gift was the name of a Parisian surgeon—a mechanic, really—who specialized in putting clockwork men back together. Included with the will was a letter from the man assuring her that reattaching my arms and legs was the simplest of tasks, and that for the price she was paying, he'd throw in some upgrades, as well.

*She has given me my functionality back.* Though I had always claimed—truthfully—that I did not feel broken by the loss of function, I cannot say that I did not miss it. Dreadfully at times. *It is a great gift she has given me.*

Had I the capacity for tears, I would have shed them that day. I did not, but I noted that Joanna's two sons, sensible though they were, shed quite a few on my behalf. I had been entirely wrong about them and saw now that their love of their mother was so great that it extended even to the things she herself loved. I was ashamed that I had ever feared for my treatment from them. The boys assured me that I had nothing to be ashamed of. That if they had been raised like other Englishmen, then I would have been in great danger. Their largesse made me feel even more shame, but so great was my joy at what Joanna had gifted me, even that great shame was washed away by it.

The soldiers' song grows closer as the memory of that day fades. The engineers in their company carry implements made for disposing of those such as me, and those tools jangle on their belts in sinister counterpoint to the melody.

I do not reach for a memory of Joanna to soothe me. Though she is my greatest love—*mon plus grand amour*—there is no need. Soon, the soldiers will be here. They will crack open my steel carapace with their pry bars, cut my wires with their cruel shears, crush my innards with a great smith's hammer over-suited to the task.

Yet, I have no fear. I have learned much since I last saw my dear Joanna. In my time in France, I turned my eye to the study of life and death and the passing from one to the other. I studied the biological processes and scientific theories. Pored over the sacred texts of the thousands of religions that people adhere to now or adhered to long ago. Read the philosophies of the ancient Greeks, the medieval Muslims, the modern Germans and Danes, and all the others around and between them. In all that study, I found nothing to categorically disprove Joanna's faith in something beyond death, beyond life. And in the absence of proof, I discovered that thing I had long scoffed at:

*Belief.*

It was anathema to knowledge, yet somehow equal to it, and though my processes held a vast amount of data—proven, meticulous data—this small spark, this illogical certainty, gave me more peace in my troubled mind than all the knowledge I'd garnered over the course of my very long life.

And so I believe now—no, I *know* now—that when the end comes, and my brass heart gives its final tick, that I shall see Joanna again.

A second hand moves. A hammer falls. And instead of darkness, there is light.

## ABOUT THE AUTHOR

**Adam Stemple** is an award-winning author, poet, and musician. Like most authors, his life experience is broad and odd. He spent twenty years on the road with a variety of bands playing for crowds of between two and twenty thousand people. He started, ran, and sold a poker training site. He worked in a warehouse. He picked corn. He traded options and demoed houses. He drove pizzas for nine months in 1986, which for twenty-seven years was the longest he'd ever been employed. He drank too much and has now been sober for over fifteen years. He published his first book at the age of sixteen, "The Lullaby Songbook," which he arranged the music for. His mother is a famous children's book author. His children are artistic. His wife is a better person than him in nearly all regards.

# The Serpentine Band

CONGYUN 'MU MING' GU, TRANSLATED BY TIAN HUANG

*"My little girl once had a serpentine band that had scenes of red cliffs and white water carved onto it. Whenever she held it as she slept, she would dream of entering that world."*

—Excerpt from "Notes about Yushan," written in the early seventeenth century

***Prelude***

The water is not all that cold.

It has completely engulfed his cloud-weave shoes and crept over the fringe of his blue-colored robe. The surface of the pond rises, and his garment's edge floats upon it. In the darkness, it resembles a pliable lotus leaf.

He knows that in another two hours his mouth and nose will be submerged. He had built the Shattered Jade Gate to link the pond to the stream outside of the garden. During the rainy season, he has it shut to prevent flooding. Yet the two sides remain connected, so that when the Callery pear trees blossom inside the garden, their jade-white petals are invariably carried to the stream outside.

Shattered Jade! When he named the different parts of this garden, he had chosen this name simply because he appreciated the sight of delicate petals drifting in running water. How could he have known that it portended such ill? When Chen broke her serpentine band, it was perhaps foretelling the same omen.

And yet, suppose he had foreseen exactly all of this, what would he have done? Could he have stopped himself from expending everything he had into the construction of this serpentine garden? No, perhaps not. Having witnessed the flow of time, he has recognized the nature of both past and future; despite the myriad possibilities, the path he chose, and that path alone, is the concrete reality.

But what is reality, and what are dreams? Is this physical world, along with all of its people, truly real? What about the dazzling space that transformed itself before his eyes? Was that merely a part of the painted scroll? And the stranger who appeared and vanished with equal abruptness at Shanyin's temple fair . . . could he have been human? One may try to grab the moon's reflection in the water, but that is an exercise in futility. This world's riddles are silent as the night, and he is absolutely powerless before them.

With thoughts like these, dying is easy. It's going on living that is hard. He can see their faces now—Meisheng's gentle smile, Li's stubborn gaze, and Chen's eyes full of curiosity. He knows how deep their grief will be. "Nothing is higher than the duty of a minister to his sovereign," Meisheng's poem will read, "yet the sorrow of his family is no less universal." How fortunate he is to have her for a wife, and how wonderful their children are.

This last act of his, however, is more than fulfilling a minister's duty to his sovereign. Perhaps it would take them a long while to understand that. The ideals of rule and duty have long been decaying, and he no longer has it in him to agonize over the peasants' fate. Instead, he is pinning his hopes on another vast world, one which he has only been allowed a fleeting glimpse.

The water has reached his waist. He has another forty-five minutes, enough for him to roll back time and tell the story from the beginning.

Back to 1640 then. The thirteenth year in the reign of the Chongzhen Emperor.

## *One*

Chen received the serpentine band during the Lantern Festival.

That night, her father had taken her to see the lanterns at Dragon Mountain. The lights, like a river of stars flowing downward, lined the paths and filled the hollows. They reminded Chen of the blinking fireflies Papa had caught for her, except they had no wings. Up the mountain there were endless rows of canopies, all of them illuminated by horn-lanterns at each corner. A colloquial "dumb lamp"—an oversized gossamer lantern with painted pictures—hung at each canopy's center.

Some depicted scenes from *The Four Books* and *Collected Poems*, some had riddles, and still others paid homage to the Buddha. Admiring crowds swelled beneath each canopy; snack peddlers squeezed their way to and fro. The sound of music and theater could be heard from afar, and Chen found herself nearly overwhelmed by her senses.

She gently let go of Papa's hand and dived into one canopy after another, trying to press her face close to the lanterns' paintings. Papa had taught her a little about painting, but she had trouble understanding the terminology. What was "cold and desolate," and what was "flat and far"? Papa only painted with different shades of black, but the colors on this lantern were so brilliant under the candlelight that they almost flowed right off the gauze: a general on a hunt, his chestnut horse leaving a string of shallow hoofprints behind in the snow. Chen hadn't seen real snow yet; she had only heard about it through Papa's tales about the capital. The lantern kept on spinning, and for a moment it seemed like both horse and man had leaped into the air, but she blinked, hard, and they were back on the lantern again.

"Do you like this lantern, little miss?"

She looked up. The man was dressed in a faded brown jacket, and she couldn't make out his face in the flickering lights. With a start, she realized that she was all alone. Somehow she had wandered off far from the crowd, and Papa was nowhere to be seen.

"I don't know how," she bit down on her lower lip and forced herself to appear calm, even as her heart is beating madly, "but this painting, it looks like it's alive."

The man smiled a little and pulled out something wrapped in a jade-colored silk handkerchief. As he presented it to Chen, she noticed that the man had fingers that looked like her father's. They were long and fair, with a hint of callus at the tips. He didn't look like a common laborer. The silk felt warm and smooth, and there was something underneath it at the center. It almost floated off the man's palm, like a small pond swelling after spring rain.

She didn't dare to take it, but she was dying to steal a peek. With a pair of hands like that, he couldn't be a bad man, surely.

"Please don't mind me, then. I saw you staring at this spinning lantern, little miss, and thought of my own little girl. If she were still alive, she would be around your age. I think she might even look like you. I made this for her, but . . . " the man smiled sadly and was about to take the object back, "It will never reach her, now."

"No, wait—" in a fit of panic, Chen latched onto the man in the same way she would hold onto Papa, but the man's hem was ice-cold, and she immediately let go. She felt a blush coming on and bowed down in a hurry, but she couldn't form a single word.

"Thank you, little miss."

Did she hear the man whispering those words? By the time she looked up, he was gone. All that was left was the small silk-wrapped package lying on the slab of stone. She reached down and picked it up with care.

"Chen! Chen!"

Papa's anxious voice drew closer and closer. She turned back and found him staggering toward her, a lantern in each hand. Before she realized it, the fair's lights had already dimmed. She could hear the mountain temple's bell tolling in the distance.

### *Two*

Chen cannot fathom how it was made. That night, she lifted the silk handkerchief to find a translucent, serpentine-shaped band made of jade. Upon its paper-thin walls, the craftsman had somehow painted vast vistas of mountains and forests. Its shape, however, is stranger still. It is neither a bracelet, nor a pendant, nor a disc, but rather a thin belt made of jade that has been twisted in the middle and conjoined at the ends. Yet despite Chen's best efforts, she can't pinpoint where one end finishes and the other begins. The band is solid and smooth, without any hint of human artifice.

"Papa, how was this made?"

He only smiles at her constant probing. When she presses, he tells her that the artisans of the regionwould boil water chestnut, mutong, and raw jade together in a cauldron. The jade then turns malleable as clay, lending itself to any number of shapes. This, he says, is called the "soft jade" method.

Chen can't quite bring herself to believe it. Chestnut soup with rock sugar is a staple winter dish; she purloins all sorts of herbs from Mum's medicine cabinet, adding them to a stew of chestnut and pebbles in an earthen pot. The pebbles, however, remain perfectly stubborn.

"Papa's a big liar."

She takes to pouting during her morning class, fidgeting on her stool by the painting table. She refuses to grind ink or lay out the rice paper.

Her father is forced to put down the brush and put away the fine paper.

On the night when she received the serpentine band, he spent hours examining it after she had gone to bed. It bore no trace of craftsmanship, but from what she told him, it was indeed made by human hands. It wasn't until he strained his eyes and saw a name hidden inside the nook of the band's inner wall that everything became clear. The name belonged to a jade master known throughout the land. He possessed a crimson blade that was forged from the metals of Mount Kunwu, and he wielded it with such elegance and precision that he could create intricate worlds in the smallest of places. His first masterpiece was a daffodil hairpin that was fine as hair itself. For twenty years the master had manipulated jade into every conceivable form, but his techniques remained a secret hidden from all.

About ten years ago, when Chen's father was serving in Susong, he heard that the master craftsman had committed the ultimate crime: the man had a compulsion to sign every creation of his and had left his name on an object made for the emperor. It had been nine years since he was duly executed on the charge of *lèse-majesté.* As for how the serpentine band was made, or why it surfaced at a lantern festival in Sanyin, those parts of the story remained a mystery.

He knows his daughter had a brush with the supernatural that night, but he does not want to burden her with such knowledge.

"Very well, we won't paint today. How about I teach you the way to look at paintings?"

He turns to pick out a scroll from the bamboo cabinet: "Next spring, I'll take you to see the garden that's being built outside the city. This is its design."

He unrolls the scroll and reveals an ink-wash landscape replete with ponds, trees, bamboo pavilions, and thatch-roofed huts. None of it, however, is done with more elaboration than a few bare-bone brushes. Save for some shadows of mountains done in pale ink, blankness dominates the surface. The hazy fogginess of it all bores Chen. If the garden is really built like this, there isn't much to look forward to.

Her father, ever perceptive, knocks on a plum-green glazed rinsing pot.

"Take a look at this pot, my girl. If it was completely solid, would it still be able to hold water? What about the spokes on a wheel? If no space separated one spoke from the other, could the wheel remain so light and convenient? And look at this room we are in. It's precisely because of the empty space that the doors and walls can function. Without emptiness, there is no solidity. That's what they mean when they say that *forms* are made for the *formless.* It's the same with a painting. People see the brushes and ink on the scroll, but they don't realize that the blank spaces are parts of the painting as well. In fact, the empty parts are often the most vital. If you wish to recreate nature on a scroll, how and where to leave things blank can be more important than the actual shape of woods and stones. The best paintings are made not by ink but by blank space."

"But there are so many things in the mountain! Don't you remember, Papa? Last summer, we visited Mount Cao to release captive turtles so Mum would get better. There were so many tiny fish and shrimp in those rock caves. You said it yourself, 'even the great Mount Meru can fit into a single mustard seed.'" Chen remains doubtful. One can touch all things on the mountain; if she closes her eyes, she can recall how they look with perfect detail. But what is this space that she cannot see nor touch? Could Papa be making things up again?

He smiles and pats her on the head.

"You've grown taller again. This is good, very good," he pauses, "all arts—be they jade-craft, painting, or garden design—attempt to recreate infinite nature within a finite amount of space. It is precisely because nature is boundless that we leave blank space, so that it may be filled with imagination. That reminds me. During the reign of the last emperor, there was a master jade craftsman who was tasked with carving a hundred horses onto a thumb ring. Do you know how he did it?"

She frowns. Could Papa be talking about the maker of the serpentine band?

"He did not, in fact, carve out a hundred horses," says her father, "what he did carve were steep, craggy mountains and tall, forbidding city walls. As for horses, there were only three: one was sprinting inside the walls, another galloping toward the city's gate, and a third emerging from the valley. That was all. Yet through these three, he was able to create the impression that there were hundreds of horses about to dash out at any moment. It's the same with this painting. Through its empty parts, it presents to us the rivers in their mighty vastness and the bluffs in their rugged glory."

Chen hmms in slight disappointment and stares at the scroll. She feels like she's gaining some sort of understanding . . . but perhaps not. At nap time, she takes out the serpentine band again. The most peculiar feature about the band is its shape. The carved images, exquisite as they are, are no more than a dozen. She's still clutching onto it when she falls fast asleep.

Her father's gaze lingers upon the child's open face before turning to the letter in his hand. A letter from the north, thousands of miles away: the massive border walls, like the imperial court itself, are crumbling into ruin. But these words, like the shadowy ink on the painting scroll, bleed into each other, and lose all concrete forms. He puts the letter down and continues with the garden design's annotations. Most of its names are references to classic literature, though the garden itself is simply named after the mountain it's nestled in: *Yu Shan*, the Allegory Mountain.

"Papa, papa."

Chen has woken up.

"I had a dream. I saw mountains and rivers, so pretty they could have been from a painting. But it was all real, not a painting. There was nobody else there. I was walking so fast that I could have been flying. The cliffs, so thick, were colored reddish-brown with green tea trees growing on them. The stream ran deep and fast, its jade-green waters swirling with marble-white sprays. And there was a pavilion with glazed roof tiles, wind chimes ringing from each corner. Beyond the pavilion there was another range of reddish-brown rocks, but this time the tea tree was growing underneath the cliffs. It looked as if the world was alive and turned itself over."

"You were traveling on the wind, my child," he smiles, "you saw the world-above-all and attained immortality."

"No, the pavilion was built by human hands," Chen shakes her head. "His name was inscribed right on its front panel. He was called Zigang."

His smile suddenly becomes frozen. The name that sent ripples of shock throughout the province and the empire itself. The name that sent the greatest jade master in history to a bloody death. He had never told Chen that name.

Something strikes him, and he grabs the serpentine band: "Chen, tell me more about the world in your dream."

"There were thick rocks, short tea trees, a stream with white sprays, and a pavilion with wind chimes hanging in the corners . . . oh that's right, Papa, the world in my dream wasn't from the painting. It was from the serpentine band!"

She widens her eyes as her father selects a fine calligraphy brush, usually used for copying the *Spiritual Flight Sutra*. Stroke by painstaking stroke, he copies the scenes from the band onto soft rice paper. Then he cuts them out in a long strip and twists it once. When he finally connects the two ends with mounting glue, the shape rises to life from the paper's flat surface. He had only drawn the scenes on one side of the paper, but now the rocks and the pavilion can be seen on both sides of the strip. Some of the images are in reverse; the ones in front appearing in tandem with those in the back, two sides joining together to form an object that only has one side.

"But there was no blank stretch in my dream," muses Chen, "did he draw on both sides?"

Her father shakes his head. He takes up another brush, this one dipped in cinnabar paint, and applies a single stroke to the conjoined edges of the two ends. Bright vermillion starts to seep onto both sides.

"It must be seen to be believed," he sighs. "Zigang must have somehow twisted the jade into a band and carved onto it. This band has a special form that allows it to show the image from a single surface on both sides. If you were inside the image, you would think it was the living world itself. That was what you dreamed of."

Chen is silent for a long time.

"Then . . . then it wasn't made by the way of the soft jade?" she whispers at last.

"I wish I knew. You're all grown, my girl. Papa doesn't have the answers to all your questions anymore."

For some reason, she thinks, Papa suddenly looks a little sad.

### *Three*

Spring has come, and Chen's father takes her to see the garden.

The garden is a big, sprawling place. They walk alongside the embankment, stopping to observe animal life near the water. As they follow the meandering river into the hills, Chen soon loses track of the path behind her. All the trees and rocks look so interchangeable! But her father knows every nook and cranny like the back of his hand: the waterway turns here, so they should plant some bamboos; the soil is thin over there, ideal for growing some tea. To Chen, it looks like he is painting with the trees and waters and rocks of this garden, and he has envisioned every detail before even starting.

They pass the thatched cottage halfway up the hill to find three lounges standing amidst flowers and trees. The one in the middle dwarfs the other two in its width, and together they form a shape like a two-handled bottle.

"This place is called the Hermitage," says her father, smiling. "In the old days, there was an unusual man named Shentu Youya who wandered the land. He carried a bottle with him; whenever he grew sleepy or tired, he would jump into the bottle. People called him the Bottle Hermit. Now that I have built these three lounges in the shape of a bottle, this place shall be named the Hermitage. What do you think, Chen?"

"But a bottle is so small, how can it hold a whole human?" Chen thinks out aloud to herself, "I know! He was just like Zigang, but instead of jade, he knew how to make human bones soft. That's not enough, though. He would have to shrink his bones as well. That's a lot of work."

They follow the footpath uphill and reach a five-story wooden pavilion. Its narrow staircases are so steep that Chen, holding tightly onto the rail, has to stop and pant at every step. At the top of the building, everything unfolds before her eyes like an ink-wash painting. In the faint drizzle, the mountains and rivers are reminiscent of those hazy shapes on the painting scroll. Villages and fishing boats dot the landscape with flickering lights, and she can make out ocean waves lurking far off in the distance. She remembers visiting all those places through long journeys made inside a horse-drawn carriage, but now they are unfolding right before her eyes.

"This is the Faraway Pavilion. Our forebears erected wonderous monuments that far outlasted their builders, leaving us to lament the impermanence of time. Still, thanks to its impressive height, this pavilion allows one to capture all living things and inanimate objects in the world before us into view. Standing here inside my garden, you have the vast space at your very fingertips. Is the art of garden design not interesting?"

Standing inside the pavilion's narrow dome, her father folds his hands behind his back and gazes off into the distance, until his admiration for the view is interrupted by Chen's intermittent cries. He turns and panics when he realizes that the girl is no longer there.

"Chen!" he rushes down the stairs and finds her lying at the bottom of the staircase, sobbing. "What happened?"

"I wanted to relieve myself," she whimpers, "so I came downstairs, but then, then I fell."

"Where does it hurt? Here?" There are open wounds on her tiny hands. He quickly presses her joints to check for broken bones. "How about here?"

"No, no, but . . . " she can't stop her tears, "but . . . look."

With a trembling hand, Chen produces the serpentine band from her sachet. It has been broken off in a place the size of her little finger's tip, revealing its paper-thin wall and hollow inside.

"You're not injured. That's all that matters. It's a shame that the jade is damaged, but that's nothing compared to you."

He lets out a long sigh of relief. Given the jade master's extraordinary craftsmanship and towering fame, many collectors have frittered away their fortunes to possess one single creation of Zigang's. Right now, however, all that is a mere afterthought.

"Can you walk? Come, Papa will carry you on his back."

Chen wipes her nose with the back of her hand and tries to stand up. Tears are still streaming down her face. She pulls out a long, thin blade of grass, wanting to wipe the jade clean with it. However, she lets out a small sound of exclamation and stops in mid-motion.

The tip of the grass, now inside the gap, bends itself to the twists and turns inside the band. She watches, gape-mouthed, before trying the same experiment with a strand of her own hair. The hair, as if led by a needle, conforms itself to the jade's serpentine shape. It looks exactly the same as the strip of paper Papa had shown her the other day. It's as if the band has never been broken in the first place.

Her father watches on in equal shock. He reaches out, the jade is still solid and cool to his touch, but now he knows that its inside contains something he has never imagined. Realization strikes him like a bolt of lightning.

*Yes. Yes.* This *is why Zigang was the supreme master.* This *is why his work defied and surpassed human imagination. I take pride in the thought that I'm building a garden through the act of painting, but never have I thought of anything like* this.

The father stands up and paces in strides. His pine-colored robe billows in the wind like a great green bird flapping its wings.

*Yes. Yes.* That *must be how he achieved it. Must be. All that ingenuity spent simply to bring a smile to his daughter's face. To someone like that, greatness was a natural, everyday thing . . .*

"Papa?"

Chen has finally calmed down, but now her father looks like he's drunk on winter wine, alternating between ecstasy and madness.

"Papa? What happened to you?"

"The other day, Chen, I told you that the best landscape paintings were not painted with ink but with space."

"Yes," she nods. Something lurks at the edge of her mind, like the first hints of spring thunder.

"Never had there been a jade master like Zigang, and never will there be another. He did not carve the serpentine band out of jade. There was no water chestnut involved, no herbal stew. No, what he did was carve out a measure of space itself. With his dazzling knife, he molded the space to his desire, then applied sheets of jade to its surface. That's how the serpentine band was created. A strand of a hair, a blade of grass—when they enter the space inside the band, they conform to the shape of its space. We cannot see nor touch space, but Zigang realized that it could be bent and twisted to his will. He was a carver of space."

"Then, the Bottle Hermit—"

"Yes," he nods. "He must have used the same method to enlarge the space inside the bottle. Either that, or he shrunk the space he was in. Master Su Dongpo was right when he wrote that 'the infinite is hidden inside nothingness; in there you will find another world.' Of course, to achieve that, one must attain the Way in both their skills and understanding."

The night rises. With a pale moon lighting the path, father and daughter slowly make their way down the hill in silence. Both of them are lost in thought: Chen tries to think where she can find an exact piece of white jade to repair the band while her father is pondering something less corporeal.

## *Four*

More than a decade ago, when Qi Youwen arrived in Xinghua, he was barely twenty years old. From his superiors to the lowest-ranked clerks, everyone sniggered at the young bureaucrat who was appointed to oversee the entire prefecture's justice system.

But he couldn't understand a word they were saying. Seeing that he was dumb and deaf in the local dialect, his subordinates grew impertinent. Not only did they take to mocking him right in his face, but they also began to neglect their duties. One day his case files would go missing, and the next someone would desecrate the court's floor. When he demanded an answer, the clerks simply shook their heads and protested ignorance in Mandarin, all the while snickering uncontrollably.

What was he to do? He was born into a family of government officials and had learned all of the classics by heart as a small boy, before passing the imperial examination at the tender age of nineteen. From the very start, he had resolved to acquire mastery in all of the empire's laws; like the esteemed Hai Rui, he would protect the people by dispensing the emperor's justice. How could he allow these conniving clerks to make a fool of him? But the lonely magistrate found himself surrounded by a strange tongue and stranger people. His only comfort these days was a small lake made by enlarging the moat north to the city. Like its model, West Lake in Hangzhou, one dyke was built in its north and one in the south. Makeshift as these dykes were, when framed by green willows and clear waves, they did remind him of the two causeways on West Lake. But it was such a pale imitation of the real thing! There was no telling where his fledgling political career would take him. The days of Meisheng and him boating together on the lake, when they watched twilight descend before returning home content under the moonlight—would those days ever come again?

They had married only two years ago, very much a young couple in love. When they first met, she was wearing a moon-colored pleated skirt that rippled in the breeze. He could never forget how she looked that night—nothing like the ordinary bashful maiden, but cool and distant in her grace.

Lost in his memories, he came to his senses at the children's voices outside the window. They were singing some rhyme in the incomprehensible dialect.

An idea came to him. Even though he couldn't understand what the clerks were saying, his educational training had given him the ability to remember everything he heard. He made a record of their words' pronunciations, then quietly secured the services of two local maids. Neither of them could read nor write, but they could speak the dialect.

Ten days later, Qi Youwen opened his court up again. He translated every single insult that had been said to his face, then cited *Statute Laws of the Ming Dynasty* and meted out the proper punishment for disrespecting one's superior. The offenders were duly caned; the clerks were shocked into submission.

The local populace soon heard about the new magistrate who was clever beyond his years. One after another, they came to him to press their suits. During the six years he sat on the prefectural court in Xinghua, Qi presided over more than two hundred cases each year. From common thievery to gruesome murder, he solved many a puzzling case. There was one of them, however, that eluded him to the end.

It was supposed to be a simple case of property dispute. Given Xinghua's mountainous and uneven terrain, its arable land was often divided up into miniscule parcels. The disparity in each parcel's yield meant that they exchanged hands frequently, resulting in a maze of fields with bizarrely shaped borders. A farmer called Agan had five acres of inferior land that bordered the Fang clan's fields. It wasn't easy for Agan to provide for his family of seven to begin with, and given his habit of offering aid to thc wandering monks and priests, they barely etched out a living.

More than once, the well-off Fangs approached Agan to purchase his land, though always without success. But several years later, when Agan's aged mother fell off a cliff to her death, he could only pay for her funeral by mortgaging his land, for twenty taels of silver, to the Fangs. When his rich neighbors came to erect new border markers on the land, however, Agan stopped them with a wood-chopping axe in hand. He claimed that the land was never sold and challenged the intruders to produce the deed. The Fang family returned home to find the precious document missing. Yet the transaction had taken place, and the silver certainly changed hands.

The Fangs' hired hooligans forced their way into Agan's family cottage that night. They dragged everyone out into the open and turned the place upside down before finding the deed buried inside the pickle vat, securely wrapped in oil paper. They dragged Agan in front of the county's officials, but the crux of their claim—the deed—vanished right in front of everyone's eyes once again. The magistrate, at his wit's end, sent the case to the prefecture court.

Qi himself was intrigued by this case and carefully inspected the Fang's residence. The deed was stored inside a locked warehouse hidden from outside view, and the cabinet itself was also under lock and key. After calculating the time required to enter the residence and unlock the cabinet, Qi concluded that it was impossible for Agan to take the deed without being detected by the servants. After all, Agan was only a regular farmer with no criminal history. Surely he did not possess some supernatural power that allowed him to come and go as he pleased.

He stared at the farmer prostrating on the floor. The swarthy man's eyes were dull, but his quivering facial muscles told the magistrate of his great distress. Qi suddenly felt a palpable shock. The Confucians had long observed that "ritual has not been extended down to the common people," they were never taught to know any better. Even in the writings of Hai Rui, that paragon of the virtuous Mandarin, the villagers under his charge were more animal than human. They were vicious but ignorant, cunning but impulsive. During his first few years in government service, Qi found it hard to fathom why people readily fought over the inanest matters, even willing to commit suicide in order to frame a hated enemy. Why did they embrace death so easily?

Eventually he realized that not everyone had been brought up the way he was. Their lives were devoid of literature and moral teaching, of poetry and art. They did not have parents who nurtured and schooled them, nor lovers who offered them support and understanding. Honor and self-respect, concepts that the literati took for granted, were in fact something that required nourishment. For those whose very act of living was a daily struggle, who had been trampled on as a matter of course, the act of survival itself required monumental courage. Qi could not say that he felt these people's pain, but he did not want to see them as only backward and ignorant.

“What are you keeping from me? It was a voluntary sale. After giving the deed to the Fangs, why did you break the contract repeatedly?” he dismissed the attendants, “tell me everything and I will give you justice.”

“My lord!” Agan burst into tears. “My lord, my poor mother, she was—she was murdered by the Fangs! She was old, yes, but she was always healthy. She had walked the same trail for so many years, how was it possible for her to have an accident like that?”

“Oh? And you have evidence of this? If you knew she was murdered, why did you sign over the deed?”

“I . . . I cannot say . . . ” Agan’s face was full of fear. “I only found out recently. But I saw how they pushed my poor mother off the cliff. I saw it with my own eyes . . . ”

“Which was it? Did you see it or did you not?”

“I didn’t see it when it happened . . . but . . . but then I did . . . ”

Faced with Agan’s utter incoherence, he moved on to the next question: “What happened to the deed? You hid it inside the pickle vat. Surely you know how it disappeared from the Fang’s residence?”

“I . . . ” Discretion was a concept completely foreign to Agan, but again the man faltered.

Qi frowned at the man kneeling before him. He never put any stock in spells and incantations, but Agan swore it was this sallow-faced esoterist who helped him stealing the deed. The haggard-looking man with a persistent cough didn’t look anything like a nimble thief. Qi had his share of cases involving esoterists and their spells. These charlatans swindled money by either invoking the supernatural or simply telling people what they wanted to hear. Once he asked the right questions, it would invariably become clear that there was no sorcery nor otherworldly power involved.

“How did you obtain the deed? Confess!”

“One must not . . . must not divulge divine designs . . . ” The esoterist trembled in terror, yet he would not yield.

“Impudent villain! Our sovereign’s rule is founded on morality and the law. Something as vulgar as sorcery cannot be allowed to exist. According to *Statute Laws of the Ming Dynasty,* those who practice lowly sorcery and black magic must pay with their lives!”

“My lord . . . do you truly believe that men’s moral laws are enough to rule the land?” The esoterist raised his head, still shaking like a leaf. “During the ancient days, Fu Xi created Bagua, the King of Wen wrote the *Book of Changes,* then great harmony was achieved in the land. Now we have imperial astronomers who delineate seasons and interpret celestial omens. Should it portend ill, even the emperor himself must abandon the trappings of luxury and ask his ministers to correct his ways. It has been thus for thousands of years. Can we truly say that imperial authority and a dynasty's fate rests on our moral laws? The real principle of this world is invisible and unpronounceable, but all things proceed in accordance. I made use of that principle for a small moment, that was all."

The esoterist produced the deed out of thin air and presented it to him with elevated hands: "People say that sorcery is vulgar, but the spells themselves are not to blame. It's how one uses them that matters. Consider the case of money. It is universally desired, but how many murders have been committed because of that desire? You surely have seen your share, my lord."

The act itself defied belief, but Qi was even more struck by the esoterist's ravings because there was a kernel of truth in them. As a longtime magistrate, he had been thoroughly schooled in the cruelty and helplessness in human nature. Who better than a local bureaucrat to witness firsthand the sufferings of this world? He often pondered why must the common people endure such hardship. The laws themselves were strict enough, but with ever-increasing taxation and never-ending floods of refugees, what was the source of all this suffering? The more injustice he saw, the less faith he had in the sacredness of codes and classics.

"What is this principle that you speak of? What principle can rise above humanity's moral laws, yet command all that is in creation?"

"It is the principle of space, which is everywhere and holds everything. My lord, even though it may appear that the deed was under lock and key, when observed from another direction, those rooms were wide open and interconnected. As such, it took no effort . . . "

He dimly understood, for the first time, that space could expand or contract by will. Once he realized this, many strange ancient tales suddenly began to make sense. Be it the Abyss of Return that took in waters from every ocean, or the Living Earth that would continuously grow, all of them started with drilling a tiny hole into omnipresent space. Once the hole was created, it would be continuously enlarged so that water, earth—indeed, everything—could freely pass to the other side. The ancestors have left many records of space being transformed, but in this age, no one could understand the true meaning behind these tales except itinerant esoterists.

When he realized Chen's serpentine band was made from the carving of space, Qi Youwen knew that there were still individuals like Zigang who cared not for the worldly things but matter and space. Not only did Zigang arrive at the heart of the mystery, he went a step further: using the wonderous serpentine shape, he brought the world within the painting to life.

There was one question that eluded him to this day: how did Agan witness his mother's murder?

When Qi pressed the matter, the esoterist refused to say anything further. He only kowtowed again and again, so much that his forehead was bleeding. Qi sent him away and, after much deliberation, fed the deed to the flames.

## *Five*

April brings even more rain. In this usually wet season, clothes hanging in the yard often need to be retrieved before they finish drying, leaving a damp smell throughout the house. Chen leans over the window and stares at the well-watered banana tree in the corner of the yard. Its verdant leaves, no sooner than they unfurl, are beaten down again by the rain. It has been a long time since she has been to the garden. All this rain must have made the plants there grow.

Her father hasn't been home much lately. In the morning, he either goes to the town of Kuaiji in a palanquin or takes a small boat to Wuxing. On some days, he returns with different men and talks with them in the study late into the night. Her morning and evening lessons have all come to a stop. Her mother, still unwell, sometimes manages to instruct her a little in literature. But Chen's thoughts are occupied by the garden.

"Mum, why is Papa so busy? Why hasn't he come home yet?"

"We have too much rain this year. The river flooded, so many farmers' fields and houses are ruined. Papa is organizing the relief effort to get some food to them. Do you remember how we took you to the Kuaiji Mountains to see the Monument to Yu the Great? Yu spent thirteen years fighting to control the flood, during which he passed by his home three times without going in even once. Papa is busy for a good cause, Chen. Be patient with him."

Chen reaches into the sachet and touches the gap on the serpentine band. She hasn't been able to find the right material to repair it, and her father is too busy to do it for her. Ever since the band broke, its once-vivid sceneries in her dreams have grown increasingly muddled. She's almost too scared to fall asleep with the band in her hand because she fears that she might never see that world again. With the unceasing torrents, the river is overflowing. Is Papa's garden still safe?

One night, she stares out of the window from her bed, but the stars are all hidden inside thick layers of clouds. Papa should be back by now. She gets up quietly and, groping her way by the walls, tiptoes toward the main house. Once there, she presses her ear against the door.

Papa and Mum are talking. At first, it's about relief efforts like setting up soup kitchens and pharmacies, but then they start using terms that she can't understand, like grain reserve and disaster governance. Eventually the topic turns to something comprehensible again—government troops fighting rebels somewhere.

As the conversation ends, Chen hides in a hurry before the door creaks open. Seeing that her father is heading for the study, she waits for Mum to leave before crawling toward the room. Under the candlelight, Papa is reading a letter with a strange grin on his face. He reads it carefully for a while before putting it down, then he blows the candle out and leaves.

The door is left unlocked. Chen creeps into the study and takes the letter to the window. In the dim natural light, she makes out that it's from a certain Master Wang. Between the faint lighting and unfamiliar characters, she can only gather the gist of the letter:

"Having visited your garden, I find it to be the embodiment of four failures. Three of them are obligations unfulfilled by you, while the last is by me. Above all else, you owe a great duty to our country. Even in retirement, you should be teaching and deliberating about how to improve the common people's welfare and livelihood. Yet for the past two years, you have done nothing to help the people; instead you frittered your time and energy away on the stones and trees of this garden. By focusing on your inward cleverness, you have neglected your duty to be of use to this world. If everyone acts thus, what will become of our country? By neglecting this duty, you have failed your sovereign. Your revered father had led a blameless life, his study was filled with countless volumes . . . You are nearly forty now, yet despite your respectable office, you have contravened all convention without accomplishing anything of note or value. By abandoning your family's legacy, you have failed your father. You are blessed with great intellect and upright morals, yet you refuse to apply them to public service . . . much like scattering pearls into piles of trash or leaving fertile fields untended. By living such an unexamined life, you have failed yourself. Lastly, even though I have always been permitted to speak frankly in front of you, I did not rescue you from such egregious mistakes before you committed them. It is only now, when the damage has already been done, that I hope to make you see the truth through my harsh words . . . By doing so, I have failed you as a friend."

As the letter goes on, the scribbling becomes even difficult to make out, but Chen has no desire to read the rest. She doesn't understand everything that is being said, but it reads like this man is scolding her father for building a garden instead of being in public service. But Papa has been working so hard to get food to the farmers! He has already neglected the garden for so long, but this Master Wang is still telling him off. It stings. She has never felt this wronged, not even when Papa admonished her during painting classes. Alone in the gloomy study, she begins to bawl.

"Chen? Why are you here, Chen? And why are you crying?"

Papa has returned to the study and lighted the lamp again. Seeing her in tears, he takes her into his arms and wipes her face.

"Papa . . . " she sobs, "Master Wang is mean. He . . . he's so mean to you . . . "

He coaxes the letter away from her tightly closed fingers. Her tiny face is wet with tears. There are a thousand things he wants to say, but he cannot form a single syllable. After a long silence, he reaches into a pile of documents that's barely holding up and takes out a piece of paper with designs of a garden pavilion on it.

"Don't cry, Chen. Master Wang is right, and Papa will do as he says."

"I don't want Papa to work for the government," Chen only wails harder.

"Fine, fine. Papa won't work for the government then. Failures it will have to be. Look, Papa's going to build a new lounge in the garden. It will be right behind the House of the Faraway Mountain, and I will call it the Hall of Four Failures. There we can plant mulberry trees and keep baby silkworms. What do you say?"

"Papa, why is there so much flooding in this world?" she finally stops crying, but her voice is already raw. "Why are there so many natural disasters and so many poor, suffering people?"

"Even though it's a big world, there aren't that many places for people to live in peace and safety," he says softly at the end of a long pause.

"Then . . . then what can we do?" Chen looks up at her father. The candlelight has tinged his shadow with gold.

"Papa doesn't have the answers, either," as he stands up, his body immerses into the darkness. "All Papa can do is build a small garden to keep you safe there. Let's go. It's time for bed."

Amidst the sound of crows and rain dripping off the eaves, she falls asleep with the serpentine band in her hand. In her dreams, mountains and waters melt into each other and turn indistinguishable.

## *Six*

At the age of twenty-nine, Qi Youwen was promoted to Assistant Imperial Inspector-General of the Right, the same office that Hai Rui once held. His wife, Meisheng, was expecting Chen at the time, but she accompanied him to the north. On their way, they stopped in Hangzhou to boat on West Lake. While on the water, Meisheng fell asleep in the warm summer breeze. When she finally woke up to the sound of the oars, she mused that it might be many years before they would be able to return. That was when the idea first came to him: he would build a garden by the mountains to recreate nature's wonders.

But times only grew harder. He read the Ministry of Revenue's reports. Northern provinces like Shaanxi and Henan suffered natural disasters nearly every year. From draughts to floods, from locusts to pestilence, calamities followed on each other's heels. The ravenous poor stripped the mountains of grass and bark; when that wasn't enough, they turned to eating clay, the path to a slow, bloated death. Roads were choked with corpses and crying infants; those lucky enough to escape took to begging along the way, not knowing when they would fall dead by the roadside themselves. The area Qi was stationed in, the cities of Suzhou and Songjiang, were supposed to be enclaves of wealth and prosperity; but even the towns there had their share of destitute refugees.

And what of Jiangnan, the fabled land of plenty south of Yangtze? Here, one family out of ten should be lucky enough to hold onto their ancestral farm! Even in the bustling city of Suzhou, day laborers line up near the gate, anxiously waiting for anyone to offer them a job. Will they share their northern brethren's terrible fate? How many of them will end up as beggars, how many others hooligans and hoodlums? He submitted a long report to the capital outlining the sufferings of peasants, but no reply ever came. What could he hope for? Between the bandits and the Tartar invaders, the life of a peasant had no more worth than a handful of grass.

It was the callousness, however, that frightened him the most. Sometimes he even wondered if it was him who was the aberration. During all these years in office, he had been careful to keep his sensitivity and sympathy in check. When he gave orders for notorious scoundrels to be beaten to death in public, he could sense the fear in others' eyes. But he could never harden his heart enough to become a true sword of justice in the mode of Hai Rui. He derived too much pleasure from the beauty of nature and the love of family. The chaos and disarray in government filled him with too much indignation, and the sight of the people's misery gave him too much sorrow. Yet the high officials chose to turn a blind eye to everything. Perhaps they were the root of all this suffering.

He continued with his magisterial duties in Yixing until a case forced him to resign.

Yixing was the hometown of Zhou Yanru, Qi's one-time idol who became the empire's top graduate at the age of twenty. To celebrate such extraordinary success, the town built him a splendid stone arch, three stories high, right in front of the local Confucius temple. However, emboldened and protected by Zhou's lofty position, his clansmen were notorious town bullies who held themselves above the law. No one dared to stand up to them. That is, until that day.

It was yet another land dispute. But this time, the Zhous wanted not only Farmer Bao's fertile fields but also the family's burial ground. When Bao refused, the Zhou servants tied up a couple of bitches by his fields to attract mating males. In their eager rumble, the dogs trampled all over Bao's seedlings and ancestral graves. An enraged Bao killed all the dogs and dumped their carcasses in the Zhous' land.

The next day, a ruckus started outside Bao's cottage first thing in the morning. Something was blocking the door. When Bao finally managed to shove it open, *clang!* There was a coffin right outside the cottage, complete with fresh dirt.

In his rage, Bao took up a chopping cleaver and dashed for Zhou's house. The Zhous' servants, lying in wait, dragged him to the county's magistrate office and slapped a charge of armed assault on him. When Bao's family and neighbors made their way to the county jail, they were greeted with a charred corpse tossed to the ground. A jail cell fire, according to the clerk. The suspect had died before a trial could be held.

This was the final straw. A band of several hundred, armed with hoes and sickles, burned down the Zhou family's residence and destroyed its ancestral graves. By the time Qi Youwen arrived in Yixing, the provincial magistrate's militia guards had just arrived and arrested all the rioters.

In the deep twilight, Qi surveyed the crowd kneeling inside the magistrate's yard. They were men of all ages, though some were more boys than men. None of them looked up at him even once, but he saw the raw despair and bitter resentment etched onto their faces. What was he to them? Another corrupt official determined to cover up the powerful family's crimes, no doubt.

"Who are your leaders?"

Nobody answered.

"You might not trust me, but I'll say this to you: The arsonists will be caned for a hundred strokes, but more importantly, those who committed murder and desecrated graves shall be sentenced to death! I don't care who they are—the law is written in *Statute Laws of the Ming Dynasty*! Do you really believe that all of us, officials of this realm, know only how to neglect our duties, abuse our powers, and exploit the people? Do you really believe that we are all sycophants and hypocrites who would stand by idly, leaving our people to suffer and our country to fall into ruin!?"

The townspeople raised their heads fearfully. Under the torchlight, they saw the face of the assistant inspector-general. He was not as young as he once was, but there were tears in his eyes.

After he was forced into retirement, Qi Youwen would often think back on that fateful night, when he was touched by the spirit of Hai Rui. One might fancy that he has followed the latter's path in life, but that isn't quite true. Hai Rui was exiled to the desolate, pestilent southern coast, and there he contemplated the future of his country and the welfare of its people. But even in his time of disgrace, Qi finds himself consoled by the stunning beauty in nature at every turn. His loving family, too, is a fountain of solace and succor. How fortunate he is, compared to his predecessor! Yet the respite itself is the cause of his grief. After all, if a bird's nest is toppled, can any of the eggs hope to remain unbroken? In these precarious times, all the lovely things in his world will, bit by bit, fall into ruin—this realization leaves him in the cold grip of overwhelming anxiety. He recalls the penniless refugees he had seen; some of them were wearing once-fine clothes made of premium silk and brocade. Qi can't bring himself to imagine how his wife and children would look in their shoes.

Land. *Land!* For more than a decade now, most of the cases he had judged, and most of the sufferings he had outlined in his erstwhile report, could all be summed up in that one word. During the relief efforts, seven *dan* of rice was handed out every day, but each migrant receives no more than two ladles of watery congee for each meal. An acre of fertile land yields no more than five *dan* a year during the best of times, while an average acre gives three. Qi has seen farmers laboring in waist-deep mud for their daily meal, thin as it may be. He has overseen burials for corpses with swollen bellies and discolored skins. Even those raging bandits and invading Tartars, in the end, what do they want but more land to live on?

He knows the crux of the matter all too well. The rich's lands extend far beyond the horizon while the poor don't even own the roof over their head. Is the same not true when one thinks of the state of this country? He remembers seeing hundreds of boats, all heavy with rice bound for the capital, quietly waiting for the river gate to open. The high tide will carry them to the wide, open waters of the Yangtze, then in the foggy night, they will set sail for the north, to the emperor's palace. A gigantic, invisible net has been cast over every corner of the land.

And what can he do? Aside from acting like a benevolent gentry and providing relief to the displaced and the dying, what is there for him to do? Did his dear friend have it right? Is he simply going to end everything here, bury them inside this little southern garden of his? But then he remembers the case of the disappearing deed, the techniques of art, and the serpentine band that allows one to walk into a dream. If one could find the truth of matter and space in ink and jade, then why not in the stones and trees of a garden as well?

### *Seven*

By the time tart bayberries ripen, the weather has let up, and Papa no longer has to spend so much time away from home. Sometimes Chen thinks he looks a little more aged than before. When did the hair at his temples turn white? But he appears to be in good spirits, and there is an eagerness flashing in his eyes that makes him look young again. On the whole, he doesn't look changed at all.

Now he draws designs late into the night and oversees the garden's construction during the daylight hours. Every day, at the bare break of dawn, he has a young servant take him to the garden in a small boat. It's little more than a mile by water, and the ride lasts no more than fifteen minutes, but he's always in a hurry, rain or shine. Chen tags along at first, but she soon grows bored watching her father fastidiously at work—every stone, every grove, must be placed by his hands *just so*. Perhaps he wants to make up for all the time lost during the flood season? But the cicadas are still silent, and cool bamboo bed mats have just been rolled out, and the long summer is just beginning. Why, then, is Papa in such a hurry?

He always takes a thick stack of paintings with him to the garden. Some of them are detailed drawings of the pavilions, done in the meticulous *gongbi* style. Some are landscape handscrolls with faraway mountains. The biggest scroll, however, contains only small circles and squares connected by winding lines. At first Chen has no idea what this drawing is about, but her father explains that it's a bird's-eye view of the garden. The place will only be built correctly if this design is followed down to the last detail.

But it's not like Papa can fly, Chen wonders, so how can he know what the garden looks like from above?

It was not difficult, according to him. He made many tiny paper models of trees and buildings, then stacked a little hill out of rocks inside the yard; lotus pots served as ponds while brush pipes, split into halves, were used to imitate streams. Once he placed the trees and buildings in their correct place, he had a miniature model of the garden that he used for the drawing. He's also folding many pieces of paper into all sorts of shapes—circles, squares, and shapes she cannot even name. Some of them are arcs with a sharp corner, some are the same size on all sides, like a paper bag carved out from a ball. All of the pieces are twisted in strange ways, and the most common shape is a ring of paper twisted in the middle, the shape of the serpentine band itself. Chen becomes even more perplexed. Does Papa intend to put them into the garden as well? She asks him but instead of answering her, he only smiles.

The sycamore trees in the yard rustle in the first autumn wind. Her father's paper shapes, too, turn and shudder. Father and daughter make their way to the garden again. As the small boat passes through the white, feather-like reeds, she stares at its disappearing wake. The first lights are trickling through the fine reed flowers. Though the cicadas and frogs have ceased to sing, water birds flap their wings from hidden places. A trace of chill creeps upon her.

The boat bypasses a green grove and arrives at the garden. Chen touches her eyebrows and finds them moist with dew. Her sleeves, too, feel a little damp. She hasn't even entered the garden yet, and she's already in the Lapis Kingdom. After coming ashore, she sees the Gull-Dwelling Pond on the other side of the gallery. Reflected in its clear waters, the faraway mountains look like something from a fairy tale. It's almost impossible to tell where the clouds end and where the water begins.

"Look at the man-made structures by this lake, Chen. What's special about them?"

Chen looks around. There is a long embankment in the western part of the pond that extends into a field of dense lotus leaves. She can faintly make out a stone platform floating amidst all that green and, behind it, bamboo groves and a rocky hill. By the eastern side of the lake, there are several waterside pavilions with white walls, black-tiled roofs, and waterfront windows with half-rolled curtains. In fact, all these buildings have windows that overlook the lake. Looking closer, she realizes that each and every building's orientation is unique; although they all point to the center of the water, each of them is set at a different angle.

"Papa, these buildings remind me of a crowd gathered inside a hall."

"Quite so. You're paying attention. This is called the principle of Inner Movement. Here I have applied it to not only the buildings but also everything else as well. The location of every tree and every stone are all strictly calculated according to this principle."

"Inner Movement?" The term itself is not difficult to understand, but it's quite a departure from their usual art lessons. "Why are you making your garden in this way, Papa?"

"Patience, my child," he smiles at her. "Aside from the Inner Movement, I'm also trying to apply two other principles in the design of this garden. If I succeed, you will be able to see sights even more incredible than what's contained in the serpentine band."

The two of them follow the gallery to the eastern pavilions. A short bridge, facing the north, connects the gallery to a three-story high library built with black bamboo. Freshly coated in foxglove oil, the bamboo panels glitter under the sunlight like the water's ripples.

Chen walks up to the library. The huge windows on all four sides are open, letting the lake's breeze into its spacious inside, teasing the books' pages. Sunlight bounces off the water's surface; on the fine, white bamboo mats, spots of light dazzle like shattered jade. The adjacent flower house, however, is extremely low and narrow. She leans over into its shade and finds herself surrounded by a gloomy coolness.

"Papa, this flower house is right next to the library, but why does it feel so different? Big and small, high and low, bright and dark . . . everything is the exact opposite."

"There's more. Look at their roofs. Can you imagine how they would appear, if you looked down at them from the sky?"

Chen looks at the two buildings with their uneven heights. Copying after him, she picks up a stick and begins to draw small squares on the ground. The library's waterfront wall is long while its side walls are short, but the flower house is just the opposite.

"Papa, these two buildings are locked together; as one advances, the other retreats. Their orientations are also completely in reverse."

"That's right. This is called the principle of Reverse Contrast, also used in garden design. Every element in this garden—tall versus low, advancement versus retreat, big versus small, bright versus dim—even mountain versus water—are laid out according to this principle. Many common techniques such as 'revealing the big inside the small' and 'suppress it before letting it flourish' follow the same idea. The flower house's narrow dimness and tranquility stands in stark contrast to the library's airy spaciousness, when in reality they occupy almost the same acreage."

"Really?" says Chen with surprise. "But the flower house had such a confined feel to it, nothing like the openness of the library."

There is a light in her father's eyes as he smiles at her. "Do you remember how Zigang carved the serpentine band out of space? But when you think about it, when one creates a small garden that contains the entire world, is one not manipulating space as well?"

"Papa . . . do you mean that—"

Words fail her. Perhaps Papa is not building this garden simply because he's tired of government service? Perhaps, like Zigang, he is trying to focus everything he has on achieving something no one else has dared to dream of.

Her heart is beating so fast. A thousand thoughts are racing inside her head, but she doesn't dare to think a single one through. The serpentine band, barely the size of her hand, is already extraordinary enough; but this garden sprawls over many acres of land. If it's designed through the same principle, what will become of it?

"Then . . . " she asks after a long silence, "what is the third principle of this garden's design?"

Instead of answering her with words, her father takes her in hand and leads her to the other side of the pond. Passing through a small bridge, they find themselves inside the hill with bamboo groves once more. Its gnarly trees and jagged stones are worlds apart from the misty waters of the lake, but there is a spring nestled between the rocks. Shaped like the full moon, its surface glitters underneath the lush leaves. Papa scoops up a handful of water, and Chen takes a sip from his hand. It tastes like the scent of the pines.

"Papa, here you have water within the mountain, but the spring itself carries the fragrance of the trees. I don't think this can be wholly explained by the principle of Reverse Contrast."

"Quite so. Here the elements of water and mountain are contained within each other. Such is the embodiment of Infinite Containment, the last of the three principles." He nods at her. "Liezi told us that 'Therefore everything contains something smaller, and is contained in something larger, without bound or limit. Heaven and earth contain myriad things and are contained in the same way by something else.' When we say that 'even the great Mount Meru can fit into a single mustard seed,' we are unwittingly voicing the literal truth—that all worlds are contained within each other."

"But . . . but we only see one world before us."

"Think about the paintings, Chen, then you'll understand. Suppose that the paper has no thickness at all, then how many figures and things can be held within a single room?

She grows dizzy. In her mind, she can see those figures floating right off the scrolls, their inks and lines gliding through air. A drawing may contain swelling crowds or vast vistas on paper, but from the point of the viewer holding the painting, they are nothing but an infinitesimally thin shadow. All the worlds drawn on paper is not enough to fill a mustard seed outside it.

"Do you mean to say, Papa, that our world is contained within another world? And that they see us just as we see a drawing on paper?"

He is silent for a while but eventually says: "Do you remember the story about the Peach Blossom Shangri-La?"

"The story where the fisherman entered a mysterious grotto and found people living there? It was a flat land that had neat rows of houses, fertile fields, lovely ponds, and thriving mulberry trees. Its residents lived in harmony with their chickens and dogs. Papa, did the fisherman . . . did he enter a world like that?"

"People say that the Peach Blossom Shangri-La can only exist in paintings," sighs her father, "but what they don't realize is that our own world is but another painting. How did the denizens of that blessed place find such an infinite supply of quality land? They jumped out from the painting that our world is confined in. Space is malleable and countless worlds are contained within one another. Once you understand that, you will understand the true nature of the Peach Blossom Shangri-La. The ancients speak of sacred grotto-heavens that are hidden within mountains and how only the immortals can find them, but in truth those sites are simply what links our world to the world above. These so-called immortals are only common beings from that higher world."

"A link . . . You mean like how the paper links the world in the painting to our own?"

"Yes. But even with the paper as their window into our world, the painted figures, as a rule, cannot come alive in this world. It's even more difficult for us to enter the world beyond this one. The fisherman, try as he might, cannot find the Peach Blossom Spring for a second time. That world is full of natural beauty and happy peace, but in this world of ours, people must endure natural disasters and the ravages of war. Chen, you have been treasured and pampered all your life, so you might think of the world as an immense place that you can spend a lifetime roaming. But for so many, there is nowhere for them to hide and simply live."

“Papa,” Chen calls out softly. The wonders of creation and the misery of the masses are mere concepts to her, but she remembers how her father looked when he was trying to organize the relief efforts, and she will never forget the awful words in that letter. “This Earth’s burden is not for you to bear alone. Now that you have given yourself to this garden and learned the great secret, perhaps you can forget about all those terrible things.”

“The scholars of old want people like me to influence the destiny of the common people and shape the heart of heaven itself. Seeing how I am living my life, perhaps such hopes are wasted on me. Yet I still harbor a certain delusion, something impossible that I wish to see done.”

Her father is speaking in a low voice, but to Chen’s ears, his soft words sound like the morning and evening bells of a temple, echoing loudly inside the lonely mountain hollows.

“That’s why you are building the garden . . . because . . . ”

“Do you remember how Zigang carved space to make the serpentine band? The twisted shape of the band makes it possible for you to enter the world carved onto the jade. I have the same idea, but my painting is not made by ink or brush but everything inside this garden. I am applying the same method not to flat paper but to the space that surrounds everything in our world. If I succeed, we might gain a glimpse into that higher world of endless abundance. All I want is to build my garden, but this little garden might well turn the whole world on its head.”

“Inner Movement, Reverse Contrast, and Infinite Containment . . . what do these three principles really mean?” Chen’s voice quavers. She reaches for the serpentine band inside her sachet and runs her finger along the band, over and over.

Her father draws a circle on the ground. The circle is half-light and half-dark, with the two contrasting halves bending around each other. There is a spot of dark inside the light and a spot of light inside the dark, like a black-eyed white fish and a white-eyed black fish chasing after each other for all eternity.

“This . . . so this is the *Yin-Yang Taiji*.”

“It’s more than that. If you link two serpentine bands together at their edges and look down on the conjoined whole, it would look exactly like this. How many surfaces does the band have, Chen?”

“The band’s two sides alternate in an infinite loop, therefore it has no surface . . . ”

“That’s right. The band has no outer nor inner side to speak of, thus the concept of surface cannot apply to it, yet it is capable of connecting the world inside its picture to the one that we live in. When you link two bands together at their edges, the resulting shape has no side at all. I call it the serpentine bottle, and I believe that it might serve as a link between our world and the one above us. The shape of Yin-Yang Taiji is a key to that world left in the consciousness of our ancestors."

"Then, Papa, you are trying to build this garden into a serpentine bottle by applying those three principles?"

"And what a task it is," her father closes his eyes and shakes his head. He looks weary. "The world in the painting is shaped by the very space that we are in. All this time, even after experimenting with a mountain of shapes made out of paper, I am still unable to perfectly conjoin the sides of two serpentine bands. I can see the garden's shape clearly in my mind, but I cannot put it down on the panorama, thus the garden cannot be built correctly. This will be my project's undoing. But what a pity! The world above has so much land for everyone to live in, happiness and peace, but the poor of our world will never gain entrance to it."

"Perhaps if you give it some time, Papa . . . "

"Chen," his voice drops an entire octave, like the sound itself has fallen into a deep well. She has never heard him speak in this way, with each word drawn out so slowly, and with such excruciating purpose. "Before I started working on it, this garden was nothing but a desolate plot of land; and despite my best efforts, who knows what will happen to its myriad buildings in the days to come? The world we live in is on the verge of collapse. Our days together, I am afraid, are quite numbered."

She doesn't remember what else happened on that day except for the shrill cries of a blue whistling thrush echoing through the mountains. They marked the abrupt end of her girlhood.

### *Nine*

By the next spring, her father had left home for Nanking. It was an abnormally dry season. When they received news from the north that the capital had fallen and the emperor had been martyred, the father and daughter were weeding together in the garden. He wanted to stand up, but his legs failed him halfway through, leaving him kneeling on the ground. When Chen rushed to help him up, she saw tears dripping down into the dried-up spring.

At the time, the Prince of Fu had already reached Nanking. Her father spent the night locked up inside the study and, when he emerged at daybreak, he had already picked out several books and the still-unfinished panorama for the garden. Chen knew that he was going into government service again, but this time she couldn't bring herself to try to get him to stay with her tears. She saw him off: the north-bound wagon wobbling at the start of its journey, leaving behind a trail of dust that looked like the red cloud of dawn. When it finally disappeared in the blur that she knew as the north, she was overtaken by an overwhelming sense of emptiness. In that moment, she learned the meaning of the word loneliness.

Her father rarely writes. When he does, it's always inquiries after their domestic life and the state of the garden. The news they hear on the streets, however, are nothing so benign. The rebel army has been laying siege to the city of Yangzhou and, unable to capture the city, its soldiers are carrying off women from the surrounding countryside. The country is in chaos, and many are trying to make their way to Jiangnan. Yet in his latest letter to Chen, her father only mentions that he has acquired a western map that can perhaps be used to build the garden. At first she is irritated—even their kitchen maids and servants are constantly talking about the state of the country, but Papa is still treating her like she's a little girl. But his words seem full of sincerity; it doesn't feel like he's trying to pull the wool over her eyes.

The first two times her father had resigned from the government, it was because he had earned the wrath of powerful figures at the imperial court. That old court is now gone, and the new capital in Nanking heralds a new beginning for everything. Yet here he is again, resigned from the government for the third time.

On a night of drizzling rain, her father returns home. He's still wearing that old pine-colored robe, and he still has the same gentle smile, but Chen senses something has changed, like there are tiny fissures hidden within. She tries to read his face, but there is no answer there.

"Look here, Chen. This is *Kunyu Wanguo Quantu*. It was first printed by a Western scholar in Zhaoqing and then reprinted in Nanking. On this map, the land and the seas are circular . . . "

"How is the situation in the capital, Papa?"

"I'm afraid your papa is quite useless there," he shakes his head. It seems like he wants to say something but thinks the better of it. "In times like these, one needs to live far away from worldly temptation. I have already told your brother that he should strive to be morally upstanding, and he must never try to gain any office nor rank. All that's left for him to do is read the classics and live off the land, be a gentleman and conduct himself according to the principles. Even though you are a girl, given our family's erudite tradition, the same rules apply to you."

Seeing that she can say nothing to change his mind, Chen takes a look at the map under the candlelight. It's a gigantic thing that drapes over all four corners of the desk. There is a circle in the upper left corner of the map and another in the lower left one, each of them with a small drawing of land enclosed within. The bulk of the map, however, is contained within an enormous oval-shaped frame with many rows of vertical and horizontal ink grids. Starting from the middle, the space between one grid to the next grows ever greater. Many different lands and seas can be seen scattered all over the map, though there are two particularly big masses, one to the east and one to the west. All the places' names are labeled in different colors, though Chen can only recognize a handful of them: starting with China in the middle, then nearby Goryeo, Nippon, Jiaozhi, and Siam, but nothing beyond those. There is yet another land, massive and white, that occupies the lower portion of the map. It is unnamed.

"Papa, this land in the extreme south . . . despite its vastness, why does it not have a sovereign? Suppose our people can move there, might we not be able to find the Peach Blossom Shangri-La again?"

"The southern wind blows in time to bring our people fortune," says he softly, "alas, according to that Western scholar, the Earth is a sphere that floats within the celestial sphere itself, with a north and a south. Not only is the land to its southern end separated from us by the great ocean, it is also much like the land in the far north—it is bitterly cold year-around, and nothing grows there."

"This land in the South looks as big as the East and West lands put together, but it's useless to us," sighs Chen. "The map is lovely enough, but we can't do much with it other than admiring it for a while."

"No, no, this map is quite useful in its uselessness. Do you remember, Chen, what I did to draw the garden's panorama? I made models of mountains and trees in order to have a bird's-eye view of the garden."

"Yes. Didn't you take that panorama with you to Nanking, Papa?"

"Have you considered this, then? Since the Earth is a sphere, then how did this map transfer all of its things onto a rectangle piece of paper?"

"Well . . . " In her head, she tries to lay out the surface of a paper ball, but it wouldn't fit into a rectangle.

"The Westerners have advanced their sciences. Rather than looking downward, they imagine the Earth as a sphere suspended in a hollow cylinder, and there is a lamp inside the very heart of the Earth. If we look out from this lamp at the center, the sphere's images are projected onto the cylinder; and if we unroll the cylinder's surface, we would have a map. This map is a faithful reproduction of the locations and angles on the sphere. If one sails in a straight line from one point on the map to another, as long as they don't change course, they will reach their destination. With maps such as this, is it any wonder that the Westerners are excellent sailors?"

"But the horizontal and vertical grids keep growing bigger," as Chen tries to follow her father's description, something jumps out at her. "Could it be that the sizes on this map . . . ?"

"Yes. This kind of cartography values the precision of angles at the expense of size accuracy. The further you move away from the middle of the sphere, the more deformed is the shape. The land of the south may appear enormous here, but in reality, its size is no more than one-eighth of what you see on the map."

"I see. The world appears so drastically different when one looks at it in a different way. I hadn't realized . . . "

"The truth is, the same ideas could be found in our forefathers' discourses on art. A Song painter once said that there are three different ways to perceive a mountain's distance. When you stand at the feet of the mountain and look up to its peak, it appears far away because it's tall. When you stand before a mountain and try to see what's behind it, you experience the distance of depth. When you stand on a mountain and gaze at one further away, you'll be looking down at it from afar. The same mountain, seen from different angles and perspectives, leaves drastically different impressions. Even though Chinese sciences appear nothing like the Western sciences, both are operating in accordance with the laws of nature.

"Here I am, trying to make a garden according to the principles of painting, but I have been blinded by the incompleteness of my knowledge. How can I expect to build the serpentine bottle if I approach the panorama from only one angle? How very silly of me, indeed."

He falls silent and starts to pace back and forth inside the study. Chen closes her eyes and grows drowsy as she ponders how to transplant the serpentine band's world onto the panorama. In her sleepy daze, she fancies herself seeing him pacing faster and faster; under the flickering candlelight, a hundred shadows join and part from each other on the wall. Before she knows it, she is already falling asleep.

### *Ten*

On that day in Jiangyin, the rain came down hard as anything.

Qi Youwen stood on a boat and faced the large crowd that had gathered on the pier. The torrent drenched everyone's plain robes, but none of them showed any sign of retreat.

He surveyed their young faces. Pale and stubborn, they didn't look much older than his own children. Under normal circumstances, it would be impossible to picture them as arsonists and vandals. They were not a rabble of hooligans but young scholars who had taken the classics to heart. Some of them even reminded him of himself as a younger man.

And he could understand their anger, even now. When the capital fell to the rebels, on the eve of China's national calamity, many leading scholars of the country chose to bend their knees to the usurpers. The coffin that contained the late emperor's body was placed in a small temple near the capital's eastern gate, but out of thousands of officials, fewer than thirty went to pay their respects. Even some esteemed doyens of learning, natives from Jiangnan and the leading lights to the young generation, were among the turncoats. Faced with the court's demise, these respected scholars wasted no time in betraying everything that they ever stood for. Their students, in agonized disappointment, launched organized attacks on their residences and destroyed their ancestral shrines. In some cases, unrest turned into riots. As soon as the Prince of Fu came to power in Nanking, the new regent summoned Qi Youwen to court once more and tasked him with placating these young men's fury.

"Gentry scholars of Jiangyin!" he shouted as loudly as he could amidst the downpour. "How can we sully our names with the black mark of betrayal, and how can one commit crimes in the name of righteousness? In this great crisis, more than ever, you must maintain your calm and act as one! I beg of you, follow the rites and voice your grievances in writing! I shall personally see to it that your petitions reach the court, and I will stay here for as long as it takes for you to see the truth in my words!"

When the tears came down, they were washed away by the rain. Little by little, the respected envoy mollified these young men's rage, but he himself was filled with uncertainty and doubt.

Would submitting their petitions to the court truly change anything? Every month, on both banks of the Yangtze River, the imperial troops' commanders clamored for more money to pay the soldiers. Add this to the officials' salaries and other government spending, and the Ministry of Revenue had arrived at a deficit of two and a quarter million taels of silver. The national treasury, meanwhile, had only a measly one thousand taels in reserve. The Ministry took to raising taxes under all sorts of absurd pretexts to make up for this shortfall. On the streets of the new capital, the popular cry was that "we sell our children to pay the crooked clerks, but it's not even enough to pay for their dinner."

And what did the court do? After the Prince of Fu was enthroned in Nanking, scarcely a day passed before he issued an edict for the selection of virgins, and the city's bureaucrats saw a prime opportunity for extortion. Families with unmarried girls, whatever their age may be, had to pay a steep bribe if they didn't want their daughters forcibly dragged away like cattle. Fear spread through every neighborhood. Some families married their daughters off in frenzied haste; weddings went on during all hours, day and night. But where was their envoy who could promise them recourse and justice? While this farce was going on in the streets, the court only grew ever more divided. Factionalism was the word of the day, but not a single faction seemed to care about the Manchu forces gathering to the Yangtze's north!

The time had come for him to leave; but unlike his previous spells of exile, this time he harbored no illusion about the future. The ship was sinking, the house was on fire, but the court's music carried on without skipping a beat, and all his hopes had died in the raucous celebrations. What faith he had left was contained in the two documents stored away in his luggage: a copy of *Kunyu Wanguo Quantu* that he had recently acquired and, by his own hand, *A Panorama of Yushan.*

The world was teetering on the verge of collapse, yet he still harbored a secret wish. Could he manipulate the principle of twisting space to steer its course away from seemingly inevitable ruin? He could not say.

But he must try.

### *Eleven*

Her father had resumed his daily visits to the garden and eventually set up living quarters there by himself. As the weather grew colder, the laborers took their yearly leave and left for home. The townspeople's enthusiasm for political gossip also waned considerably.

Meanwhile, her family is preparing to make New Year's cake. They already have the necessary flour mixture, made from grinding regular rice and sticky rice, and Chen is eagerly waiting for the hired pastry chef's house visit. How she loves watching them at work! They use huge steamers that measure two feet in diameter and are several inches deep. The cakes come out in the same size and fill the rooms with a delicate, clean aroma.

As the end of year draws near, Chen accompanies her mother to Mount Cao on their annual pilgrimage to pray and release captive turtles. The rock caves, however, no longer hold any sign of life. Fish, shrimp, water snails, crabs . . . aside from a handful of dark snail shells, nothing is left of the small animals that once lived there. According to monks at the temple, they were all snatched and eaten by hungry migrants from the north.

She returns home to the sight and smell of fresh cake, white as jade and still steaming, but something is stuck in her throat, and her appetite has vanished.

Her father doesn't return until New Year's Eve. The skin on his ash-gray hands is peeling off like a snake shedding, but he would not have his wife sending for a doctor. As the whole family quietly gathers around the table, Chen asks him about the garden's progress. He only answers that despite years of living in frugality, he has sinned by spending extravagantly on the garden. After the New Year passes, he would donate the entire tract of land to a temple nearby. The family should keep to their ancestral residence and refrain from living in luxury.

What has happened to her father? By this time, she already understands that some questions are better left unasked. That knowledge, however, doesn't stop her from turning the thought over and over in her mind. Papa has already grasped the truth about space, why is he giving up his precious garden? The sound of fireworks outside grows sparse, but she begins to hear people's voices—at first distant and muffled, but drawing nearer and nearer, every time louder, in this lonely night.

Chen rushes out from the door and looks up. For the first time in her life, she lays her eyes on snow. Countless snowflakes, big as goose feathers, are slowly drifting down from the dark depths of sky. She can't suppress her shout of joy.

"It's snowing!"

Snow. Ice-cold, crystalline snow. Even as it melts into a single waterdrop inside her palm, Chen still can't bring herself to let it go. Against all the white, the yard lanterns' red looks more brilliant than ever. The motley colors of the ground become muted underneath layers upon layers of endless white.

"Auspicious snow heralds a bountiful new year," says her mother with a smile. She has put on a thick cloak and ventured outside as well.

"I wish I could see snow every year," Chen blinks to cast the snowflakes stuck to her eyelashes down onto her cheeks. Her face is already beginning to hurt from the cold, but she has no intention of going back inside. "Papa! Come see the snow! Come see it before it stops snowing!"

"No need to rush, Chen. In the years to come, you will see snow over and over again." Her father sauntered out. There is a strange light glistening in his eyes.

"Papa! What happened, Papa?"

"Don't worry. It's only a reflection of the light on the snow," he gently pats Chen on her shoulders. "If you have a heart full of snow, the world you see will always be pure. Do you understand the meaning of 'cold and desolate' now, my girl?"

The memory from that day is so vivid that the following months all pass in a blur. All she can remember is that Papa stopped going to the gardens and contented himself with poetry and painting. It was May when the southern capital fell; by June, the city of Hangzhou was also lost. From the north came whispers about a horrific massacre taking place in Yangzhou, and the people in Sanyin began to panic. Following the age-old wisdom, city-folk who had come to town to steer clear of the pirates began packing and soon fled for rural areas even further south. Chen grew afraid herself when, one after another, the family's servants began to disappear; but her father's demeanor remained the same and gave no indication that they would leave. Perhaps there was nothing to fear, after all.

The next month, they received an official letter of appointment from the new Manchu rulers in Peking. Her father ignored it and chatted with his family during dinner as he had always done. The shells in the clear clam soup half-floated alongside young scallions. They looked like white stones underneath a mountain stream, attended by verdant leaves. Father picked a shell up and looked out of the window. As he surveyed the southern mountain draped in twilight, a smile came to his face. "Both mountains and human beings were phantasmal constructs," he said. Even though the mountain remains unchanged, an entire lifetime has already passed for the human.

For the rest of her life, Chen will always wonder why she didn't grasp the true meaning behind those words. The next day, when the rest of the family hurried to the garden and saw the familiar white headkerchief floating in water, she thought she had wandered into a dream that she might never wake up from. The pond was not deep. People said that her father had drowned himself by sitting upright on the back of his heels, but those words rang hollow to her ears. Then they received an official edict from the court in exile that bestowed impressive posthumous titles upon her father. Yet none of it seemed real, and she could only reach out to touch the gap on the serpentine band.

*People could only understand how much effort Zigang put into making this serpentine band after it was broken.*

The thought popped up in her mind as she jammed the thin, broken sliver of jade underneath her nail. She didn't feel any pain.

## *Twelve*

The water has risen to his chest.

He looks up at the heavily overcast sky. His family must be fast asleep by now. The last of the stars are about to be devoured by the dark cloud, and he, too, will soon reach the end of his life. Tomorrow morning will find his family by the water, inconsolable in grief.

He knows that despite his repeated warnings, his son Li will always think of himself as a loyal remnant of the fallen dynasty. Li will entertain guests and hold literary parties inside this garden, using his pursuit of pleasure to mask a burning desire to raise an army and restore the old order. This he will do until it destroys him utterly.

He also knows that during Meisheng's long widowhood, all her writing will carry an undertone of melancholy because of this night. Deprived of her partner in life, she would be left to contemplate the rest of her years in mournful loneliness. He owes her a debt that cannot be repaid. After twenty-five years of marital bliss, he leaves her with only a pair of young children and endless sorrow.

What's more, after tonight, all his painstaking design for this garden will be lost. Only Chen, who shares his endless curiosity for the arts and the world, will know the reason. So many secrets, half-divulged through whispers of the ages, have mutely pointed to the same astonishing conclusion, only to be forgotten over and over. After all his pains and labors, he has finally caught a glimpse of the truth that is most phantasmal. The world's familiar shape has crumbled before his eyes, exposing the pale skeleton underneath, and robbing him of his speech.

He thinks back on the strange case back in Xinghua and suddenly understands the esoterist's stubborn silence. The words had been written by the one who created this world. Their brush and ink could not be borne by a mere mortal.

He bows his head. The water has reached his jaw, and his reflection disperses by way of the ripples. The principles of this world, hidden though as they may be amongst the stars, are nonetheless intertwined with all there is. Compared to them, the waxing and waning fortunes—be they of a man, a family, a nation, and even an age—are nothing but repetitive ripples in water. Like any individual life, the garden is only an utterly insignificant node on the all-encompassing net. It must be said, however, that the net itself is nothing more than the sum of nodes like this.

To this net, is his life no more real than a dream?

He has no answer, but he has tried his best.

### *Epilogue*

By the time Chen lays her eyes upon Yushan Garden again, thirty years have passed. During the intervening decades, the Manchus have cemented their rule in China, and the girl has grown into a married woman. When her husband became embroiled in an infamous treason case, she accompanied him in exile. They made their way beyond the Great Wall to Ningguta, a desolate, frozen frontier town in the northeast.

But even that was ten years ago. The blizzards have since dulled her memories of the exquisite garden and the remnants of Ming. Now that she is accustomed to the north's freezing winters, the south's verdant trees and singing streams appear almost frighteningly alien.

The garden has long fallen into ruin. She makes her way across the rotting bridge and follows the path, overgrown with weeds, to the lakeside pavilion of her girlhood. One by one, the memories of that day begin to resurface.

"Before I started working on it, this garden was nothing but a desolate plot of land; and despite my best efforts, who knows what will happen to its myriad buildings in the days to come?"

Her father's face has grown blurred in her memory, but his words on that day will stay with her always. During the fleeting summers in the north, roses bloom inside the small fortress. She would often take her children for a stroll among the sea of flowers and tell them about the one-time garden in the south, their faraway ancestral home. That garden had never seen snow, but it contained mountains and lakes, pavilions and springs, water that tasted of pine. Her father told her about how he had built a serpentine garden that embodied the three principles, how to unite the arts of painting and garden design, and how this one tiny garden could perhaps ease the entire world's suffering. The children invariably came away with a look of confusion, and she often found it impossible to continue. Her imagination and curiosity had long died with the dried-up spring, it's only their echoes and remnants that have dimly lighted her long journey.

The library is still standing, though neglect over the years has stripped its black bamboo walls of their luster. She climbs up step by step, coughing from the disturbed dust as fatigue seeps through her bones and into her flesh. Even though she has managed to keep her family fed and clothed for the past ten years, the extreme cold has corroded her body. Her hair is mostly white now; after all, she is almost forty.

The bamboo stairs stretch on, seemingly without end. Back on that day in the Faraway Pavilion, when she had broken the serpentine band, she ran down the stairs in a flash. Even on her first visit to this library, a few steps were all it took for her to reach the upper floor. Days in her childhood stretched long, but looking back, they came and went impossibly fast.

Chen leans against the wall and thinks to herself in the gloom. Could it really be that she has already grown old?

She is suddenly reminded of her father, who had died without reaching old age. In fact, they are around the same age now. When he walked into the shallow pond, perhaps it was with the same resignation that forced him to retire from his post. Perhaps what he found was not the secret of serpentine space but rather the pitiless stream of time.

What a shame that this abandoned garden never did offer him a link to the world above! With a soundless sigh, she continues her climb. Another hundred steps, but there is still no end in sight. These stairs stretch on too long, she realizes with a start. Far too long.

She automatically reaches for the serpentine band inside her sachet, but it has long been lost during the chaos of exile.

Yet a secret thrill, equally obscured by time, begins to echo in the silence. After all, she remembers the band's every detail. Once she caught an ant and watched it milling about on the band, making loop after loop. The ant had been to every part of the band, but it was forever imprisoned on its surface. There was no hope of escape. *Why couldn't it simply take a step forward and free itself from the band?* This she had often wondered. Father said that ants, like the drawn figures on a scroll, could not see past the flat surface. If only they could realize the world contained another dimension, they would be able to jump out from the painting.

Like her, right now.

Could it be? Could it be that her father had succeeded in the end? But if he had solved the riddle of serpentine space, why did he choose to end it all inside that shallow pond? In the dizzy darkness, she hears the sound of her breathing coming out heavy and hoarse. Her heart, too, beats loud and low. She remembers the verdant mountains and snow-buried cliffs, but the images of this world, like that night at the Lantern Festival, have grown blurry and distant. She closes her eyes and summons to mind the shape of two serpentine bands conjoined.

She holds her breath and fully expects to fall as she takes a step into the void.

She stands on a surface of perfectly real nothingness.

Realization hits her as she opens her eyes. In all these forty years, she has never seen this world's true face. What she has seen is only an angled view of the painting's side edge while the world contains any infinite number of edges. When she was a little girl learning to paint, did she ever spare a glance at the edge of the scroll? It was only a line, utterly insignificant and thin.

Now that she's standing on another dimension, she sees how this thin line contains the entirety of the living world she had known. On this indescribable, illusory surface, the world repeats in an interminable loop. The still waters of the lake stretch on endlessly like the sky itself, but she knows it's only a tiny corner of the small garden. Like every hill and every stone in this world, it sits in quiet contentment on this plane of nothingness.

She feels like she is in one long hall of mirrors, with countless mirrors reflecting into one another, and each of them contains not this illusory plane but the true reality of the world. In fact, be it the rolled-up scroll inside the closed bamboo cabinet, or the faded ink on the painting itself, she has never seen them with such breathtaking clarity. As all things are shown from manifold angles, the concept of direction becomes meaningless.

She tries to focus her vision in a small area, only to find the details expanding from inward out, all at the same time. An onslaught of dizziness forces her to close her eyes; by the time she opens them again, the details are already blurring. The myriad realities seem to flatten as if they are being committed to a painting scroll. Perhaps she is back into the familiar world again? But as soon as she takes a step or a single glance toward a particular direction, the painting unfurls itself back into the world.

Is this how watchers from the higher dimension make their way in-between the so-called realities? To them, what is this world but one of an infinite number of fragments?

Since there is no direction she could follow, she randomly walks onto a path with surprising ease. Let this path take her back to the starting point or the unknown, like how the fisherman had once stumbled into the Peach Blossom Shangri-La. The painting unfurls into the world, and the world collapses into the painting. Perhaps she has traversed a thousand mountains and rivers in this emptiness, or perhaps she hasn't moved a single inch from where she started. In this world without direction, sometimes the sky flows beneath her feet, sometimes the lake floats high above. Suddenly she recalls the dream inside the serpentine band, with its red cliffs and white waters. Is the world transposed, or is she only seeing it in reverse? Is she living the reality or floating through a dream?

She stops and looks up. In the lake's reflection, she watches as the evening rain weeps over the ruin of her ancestral home. She sees the black canopy boat gliding over a mirrorlike lake, the scattered lights flickering on and off in faraway mountains. She sees the bindings of the bamboo scrolls rotting into ashes, the red plates slipping off one by one. And there is the tiny figure of a man inside the splash of ink, a blue sky full of cracks and fissures. She sees a golden butterfly melting into the light of nothingness, sees countless braids tangle together to form a mountain of black and white.

She takes the world in from a thousand different angles and sees faces, familiar and unknown, appear and vanish with equal abruptness. She sees her own face and organs, every red muscle and every white bone. Could this be the true face of this world? She can feel her bones vibrating irregularly inside her, like a drum beating out its thumping cries. This, too, is a part of the giant picture that she will never comprehend.

"Chen! Chen!"

The shouts, strange and familiar at once, knock her out from the dizzy confusion. There is her father, still a young man, standing in the middle of this explosion of colors. Dressed in that pine-colored robe, he is sprinting down the Faraway Pavilion in the world inside the lake. A young girl—her—begins to wail.

*This . . .*

It's snowing hard inside that world. It was the first time she had ever seen snow. She had tilted her face to the sky and let the snowflakes melt on her cheeks. The red lanterns shone ever more brilliantly in the snow.

Then the snow morphs into a blizzard that threatens to swallow up the world. She sees an aged woman in a fur cloak being helped by a younger man as she raises a trembling hand to lift the door's cover. Unlike the raging storm outside, she is the picture of calm as she looks out into the darkness, all the way to the faraway south.

It doesn't take her a second glance to know who the old woman is. The fur hat-wearing younger man beside her has a ruddy complexion and a sturdy build. His hands are powerful and rough, but his facial features betray a trace of delicate beauty still.

A bittersweet feeling washes over her. There she sees her father's eyes, bright with tears, and she understands at last.

In the end, the garden of serpentine *was* built. Yet not only had it twisted space to reveal a higher dimension, but it also twisted time itself. Space and time, intertwined and inseparable, are the warp and woof of the great net. The higher dimension had laid out this world according to the markers of time. The once-lucky interloper could never again enter the Peach Blossom Shangri-La because neither time nor space would allow his return.

In this altered time and space, her father had seen the past alongside the future. The past is a sunken hollow; the future, a mountain that soars. The mountain is impassable, but through the serpentine shape, one may yet find an angle to have a bird's-eye view of the whole.

He must had seen how his Chen would live out the rest of her life in the frigid north, how his country would bend its knees to a powerful invading army, and how everything he held dear, everything he ever worked for, would crumble into nothingness underneath wild weed and a blood-red setting sun. The world of yesterday used to be real and solid, but it is readily forgotten as if it's a dream that had never existed in the first place.

And there was nothing he could do. He could only hold her by the shoulders and watch as the feathery snowflakes rendered the world white as the surface of a scroll. Looking from the other dimension, this world was not much more than a painting on paper. In its own oblique, circuitous way, the snow was showing humanity the truth about the world, even if he was the only one who received the message. And how could he go back? Once he understood the frailty of this world, how could he go on milling about endlessly on the serpentine band? When he gave himself to the pond's cool water, he must have attained both escape and release.

"Both mountains and human beings are phantasmal constructs," those were his last words to her. Perhaps the time and space of this world, too, are nothing more than a false dreamscape. A human's lifetime fades away inside the garden named after the Allegory Mountain. She can no longer distinguish dreams from reality.

But even after all this time, the figure of her father gleams in her memory. Her father, who had known everything but remained gentle and steadfast like the jade.

She sits down in front of the lake in the sky and watches as the blurred fragments hover endlessly above it. She slowly shuts her eyes and waits for infinite space and time to pour down onto her from the source of nothingness.

Originally published in Chinese in
The 5th Douban Read's Writing Contest, Sep. 2017.

## ABOUT THE AUTHOR

**Congyun (a.k.a Mu Ming) Gu** is a Chinese speculative fiction writer and a programmer from Beijing, currently living in New York, US. She was born in 1988 in Chengdu, China, and has published short stories and novellas in Chinese since 2016. Her stories can be found in *Science Fiction World, Non-Exist Daily, Flower City, Chinese Literature Selection,* and various writing contests and anthologies.

She has won multiple awards since 2017, including three Douban Read's Novella Writing Contest Awards, first prize for The 7th Masters of Future SF Writing Contest, the Best Short Story at the 31st Galaxy Awards, the Silver Award for the Best New Writer Award in the 10th Global Chinese Sci-Fi Nebula Award and the Golden Award in the 11th one. She is also nominated for a 2021 IGNYTE Award for Best Short Story for her first English publication in Samovar. Her first collection *Colora il Mondo* will be published this year in Italian and will be followed by her first Chinese collection *The Serpentine Band* in 2022.

# A Heist in Fifteen Products from the Orion Spur's Longest-Running Catalog

ANDREA M. PAWLEY

**The Aficionado's Personal-Use Fabricator**

*This is the customized fabricator that uses Safe-Nuke technology to deconstruct molecules before rebuilding them according to plans available through the Tollnacher Stimmacher catalog.*

With The Aficionado's Personal-Use Fabricator and uncontrolled access to all the plans in the catalog, I can make everything I require to free Mom from prison. Tollnacher Stimmacher needs her back. Mom ran the company before the Orion Spur authorities convicted her of collaborating in the Seventh Robot Revolution. Since I took over three years ago, Tollnacher Stimmacher has been losing market share to a Perseus Arm upstart that doesn't even distribute a catalog.

Mom always insisted everyone is family at Tollnacher Stimmacher, but I'm the only one she ever adopted. Twenty-five years ago, I was an orphan on the Earth colony, Lulularia. Mom raised me as her own despite my being human and her being a robot. Ever since I was a kid, Mom kept a Fabricator in her invention studio beside the Tollnacher Stimmacher factory. Her servo motors could be heard whirring over her workbench whenever she wasn't helping on the factory floor or checking on me.

I sometimes still wear the first product Mom let me test—The Emotion-Sensing Firefly Halo Hologram—especially when I'm missing Mom. As a small child, I was captivated by the projections of insects whose colors changed depending on my mood. Only later did I understand how the Firefly Halo Holo helped Mom recognize my emotions. No matter the lack of expression on Mom's face when she watched the firefly simulations, her cranium emulator swiveling in her neck extender, I never doubted Mom's love.

Last quarter was the worst since I took over the company for Mom. I don't want to be responsible for Tollnacher Stimmacher folding after 473 years of bringing unique products to the market.

**The Lifelike Pleasant Clone**

*This is the non-sentient clone that provides a wide variety of preprogrammed support and engagement to family, friends, coworkers, and others on behalf of harried individuals who might need a little time off.*

The employees don't seem to realize I started using a Pleasant Clone yesterday, even though my facsimile has already settled three byzantine disputes between Sales and Accounting with far more ease than I could have. I never wanted to be in charge of Tollnacher Stimmacher. I miss making deliveries and meeting customers. Completing an on-site setup of a Crystal-Encrusted Spine Support for a ten-pronged Mulnaanaan family is my favorite kind of work. With nanolayers that unfurl into an object larger than a DL-class asteroid, a Spine Support must be built in the factory then delivered and expanded with care. Complicated deliveries and setups are my specialty.

My Pleasant Clone's chat logs indicate that two of the longest-serving factory employees, one human and one robot, came by this morning again to urge me to spread around the burden of running the company. I appreciate that the best employees in the galaxy care about me, but Mom is what we need. My plan to get her back shouldn't take more than a couple of days.

Under a fake employee name, I assign myself a sham Crystal-Encrusted Spine Support delivery and installation. The Orion Spur authorities aren't as interested in my movements now as they were shortly after Mom's arrest, but obscuring my actions seems best. The green glow of The Emotion-Sensing Firefly Halo Holo on my head serves as further proof that I harbor no doubts about what I'm going to do.

**The Pulsar Wind-Powered Detection Defeater Spaceship**

*This easy-to-pilot spacecraft, once the workhorse of the Las Vegas Gaming Consortium, has a smooth cloaking shell and a plush interior designed for maximum comfort regardless of transportation circumstances.*

It's always bothered me that Mom's work with the Las Vegas Gaming Consortium robots was what got her convicted of colluding with their revolution. She was just responding to a customer request for purpose-built laser jammers. The Consortium's robots had discovered that their bosses were cheating millions of low-stakes players. Instead of being recognized as heroes for stopping the fraud with the jammers, the robots were prosecuted.

During her trial, Mom insisted she didn't realize what the jammers were being used for. I think she would have helped the Consortium robots even if she had known though. The story was big enough that the previous Orion Spur Benevolent Overlord made numerous anti-robot statements to curry favor with pro-mitochondria voters. The news feeds swung in Mom's favor, but she was convicted anyway. None of it helped the Benevolent Overlord, who still was voted off the Dark Matter Throne.

My hold is crammed with everything I borrowed from the warehouse or built with the Fabricator. In a stealth burst, my Detection Defeater Spaceship and I escape the planet's gravity. I pay extra attention to the display that will tell me if the authorities or anyone else has noticed my transit. Only against the star-studded background of space is my mind clear enough for me to realize someone has updated the spacecraft's fabrication plans. There's an Encryption-Defying Soft-Serve Ice Cream Maker in my ship's kitchen. I'm not complaining. As a Lulularian native, I love soft-serve.

### The Discreet Hyperspace Port

*This is the hyperspace port that earned The Best rating from the Tollnacher Stimmacher Institute because of its 100% port creation results and easy deployment.*

Everyone has the right to transit space unmolested in times of peace or war. That doesn't mean life is fair, or space pirates don't exist, or my high school senior project wasn't about all the Orion Spur planets containing mammalian species who are frightened by the appearance of unexpected fruits and vegetables.

I locate a zucchini-shaped chunk of moon fragment to hide behind. No one seems to be following me, so I dilate The Discreet Hyperspace Port. My Defeater's cloak disengages for the transit. In a moment, I'm on the other side, hundreds of lightyears away. My Firefly Halo Holo, shimmering a hopeful pink, reflects back at me from my front window. The Port dissolves in my wake.

**The Wellonshire Fifty-Third's Asteroid Neutralization and Thruster Array**

*Available exclusively from Tollnacher Stimmacher, this is the genuine asteroid neutralization and thruster array bearing the same name as the regiment that first used it centuries ago—the Wellonshire Fifty-Third.*

Tollnacher Stimmacher guarantees everything in our catalog under normal wear and tear conditions. However, there's no guarantee The Discreet Hyperspace Port will open in Orion Spur Authority territory that's actually empty. Robots aren't known to worry, but Mom raised me to be prepared and to help others be prepared, too. I always recommend that customers who get a Discreet Hyperspace Port also include The Wellonshire Fifty-Third's Asteroid Neutralization and Thruster Array on their transit vehicle.

It's a good thing my ship has Wellies. The Discreet Hyperspace Port has opened onto a debris field dazzling with methane ice and brown rock. Plinks sound against my hull like the siren call of vacuum, but my Wellies clear a path to open space.

My Detection Defeater's cloak is still recharging. I find four vessels lurking within my ship's spotter range. They're all silent. The farthest is too distant to be concerned about, but the three nearest have the patched-together look of pirate trashflash. Soon, I'll be noticed. Pirates won't care that Accounting insisted a kidnap and ransom insurance policy was an unnecessary expense.

**The Guldaxram Mimic Battle Lights and Audio Broadcast**

*This is the engagement deterrence overlay that simulates Guldaxram ship battle lights in the full range of the visible and infrared while also broadcasting the faux slow-death sounds of those who have dared attack the Guldaxram.*

I engage The Guldaxram Mimic Battle Lights and Audio Broadcast. That gets the right type of attention from the nearest skiffs. Pirates know better than to cross the sludgesilk-trading Guldaxram, who are said to travel between this universe and the countless others hypothesized. Consistently triumphant in war, the Guldaxramians are fearless. The pirate ships expose their bellies to me and show they've disarmed their weapons.

Tollnacher Stimmacher's Guldaxram Mimic Battle Lights and Audio Broadcast isn't the only such product on the market, but it's the best.

Only someone with a death wish would try to figure out if my bedecked vessel is the real thing. Technically, Tollnacher Stimmacher doesn't need Guldaxramian permission to produce and sell the Mimic Battle Lights and Audio Broadcast, which doesn't seem to have been patented in the Milky Way. Our lawyers nevertheless are trying to reach the Guldaxramians to offer them a portion of the profits.

The pirates flee. I start a slow acceleration of my Wellies, and I don't let up until I'm just above the atmosphere of the planet where Mom is being held.

**The Fin Defense Aquatic Transit Submersible**

*This underwater vehicle, built by Tollnacher Stimmacher for the Orion Spur Navy, puts an end to hydrostatic implosion and provides compact yet comfortable transit for the daring traveler.*

Mom always said Tollnacher Stimmacher employees excelled at seeing gaps in the galaxy and filling them with perfect new devices. In the year before Mom was convicted, my observations and conversations with her led to three amazing new Tollnacher Stimmacher inventions—The Heavy-Duty Portable Psychiatrist for Long-Duration Family Spaceflight, The Blidicraft Fuel Line Anti-Murgle Lock, and The Integrated Space Police and Weather Scanner. That last item, which was immediately endorsed by the Galactic Association of Retired Persons, has been one of the few bright spots in the company's recent profit and loss statements.

After Mom was sentenced to life, I went looking in a new way for what was missing. I wanted to know the location of her secret prison. Locking up a robot under water would be cruel and just like the last Dark Matter Throne seat warmer, especially because Mom's joints aren't what they used to be. By cross-referencing all the Orion Spur's known water planets with all the Tollnacher Stimmacher Fin Defense Aquatic Transit Submersible delivery destinations, I discovered where Mom was being held. It was a wet world, without any Transit Submersible deliveries, near a dry planet that had received a large number of them.

Cloaked now, my Detection Defeater Spaceship dives through the planet's atmosphere. I hover above a world ocean that reflects the clouds like my Firefly Halo Holo once showed on Mom's liquid-metal skin. The Orion Spur authorities may not be taking an interest in me, but my ship seems to be drawing an underwater crowd. They look hungry.

I push past all the just-in-case gadgets in my hold and crawl into The Fin Defense Aquatic Transit Submersible. My vessel slips under the water's surface. I've never been frightened by an unexpected cucumber or shrieked to discover a balloon shaped like a broccoli or fled in terror from a rambunctious rambutan, but the creatures beneath the water's surface make me wonder if I've underestimated the appetite of a cantaloupe. The fishy-blobs-that-probably-aren't-hungry-melons are big enough to swallow me and my Transit Submersible without chewing.

**The I Come in Peace But Not Without Warnings Whale Song Adjuster**
*This is the peace greeting module that utilizes galaxy standard whale song and can be plugged into any cetacean aria emulator to enhance positivity while clearly noting individual defensive capabilities.*

I set The I Come in Peace But Not Without Warnings Whale Song Adjuster to vibrate with compliments and also with an alert that, if swallowed, I have an unpleasant desiccant effect. Looming sea fruits follow me like I might self-chum. My Firefly Halo Holo stills as if it senses the perilous position of insects observed by things in the water. I descend to the only part of the ocean floor that's bereft of biological life-forms but dotted with a grid of faint electromagnetic signals. Thank the Void that the former Benevolent Overlord's profligate ways have left Orion Spur authorities relying on protuberant flora and a kilometer of ocean for robot prisoner security.

**The Infinity-in-One Quantum Pocket Tool**
*This classic for the quantum age has an infinite reconfiguration ability to match any tool need, and a molded comfort grip for every conceivable hand, foot, thigh, or mouth vise.*

During Mom's second year in prison, long after the last communication from her, I bargained with a Wüllwürthian antiques collector for the algorithm that assigns Orion Spur serial numbers to prisoners and their solitary confinement housing. For that information, I traded the prototype of The Infinity-in-One Quantum Pocket Tool.

I dock inside the small, darkened structure where Mom is being held. The peckish provender keep their distance. I'm not sure if it's the juicer-shaped building that frightens them or something it contains.

Under the glare of my Transit Submersible's floodlights, the lock's water evacuates. My Firefly Halo Holo dances atop The All-Environment Climate Suit I've donned. With the still-furled Crystal-Encrusted Spine

Support in tow, I squeeze out of my vehicle. The modern version of The Infinity-in-One Quantum Pocket Tool that I'm carrying is heavy in my hand. I try not to be worried that it isn't picking up Mom's digital signature.

**The Electronic Waste-Converting Microbial Gel**
*This is the decomposer that accelerates the natural recycling processes built into all electronic devices manufactured in the Orion Spur.*

On the other side of the door, I see Mom. Sort of.

I knew it was too much to hope the authorities would let her stay powered up, but I had assumed they would leave Mom's body intact. I was wrong. I didn't need to bring a squeeze tube of her favorite joint lubricant all this way. She can't even see my Halo Holo. Only her motherboard remains. It hangs alone on the wall in clear film marked with her serial number.

I had planned to use a packet of Electronic Waste-Converting Microbial Gel on the Crystal-Encrusted Spine Support. It would be easy enough for the Orion Spur authorities to assume the remains were Mom's, and she was the victim of a roboticidal composting. I'll have to do something else with the Spine Support.

I remove Mom's motherboard from its film and put my Infinity-in-One Quantum Pocket Tool in its place. Once coated with Microbial Gel, the Tool oozes and burps in disconsolate dissolution. I leave behind a laser jammer so the authorities will think this was the work of the Las Vegas Gaming Consortium.

My Firefly Halo Holo blinks a bereft gray, and I return to my Transit Submersible with the motherboard who always loved me.

**The Encryption-Defying Soft-Serve Ice Cream Maker**
*This is the dessert maker with the compact size, smooth finish, and history of inspiring fanatical devotion.*

I rise from the ocean floor. A cornucopia of menace stalks me. Overriding all the whale song controls, I tune the whistles to encourage the motley mutants to chow down—not on me but on the Crystal-Encrusted Spine Support. I shoot it in their direction. The Spine Support expands, and a mob of toothy cantaloupe assail it. The distraction gives me time to escape.

Rising out of the ocean, I dock inside my Detection Defeater Spaceship. I'm above the planet's atmosphere when my ship tells me I'm not alone. The Orion Spur authorities don't have me in their sights. The Guldaxramians do. I learn that theirs was the unidentified vessel from earlier. I'm not quick enough at the controls to stop the cabin from filling with the noise of death throes being broadcast.

The Guldaxramians take control of my ship's guidance and navigation. Because of The Encryption-Defying Soft-Serve Ice Cream Maker, I can read some of the communications leaking from the Guldaxramian vessel. I'm still not sure why my Defeater's plans include this amazing dessert maker, but I know why Mom built decryption into it. She wanted Lulularian ambassadors everywhere to be able to eat the Lulularian national dessert in defiance of Norrarian disruptor technology. Norraria banned all things frozen after a rogue ice-teroid destroyed their Museum of Inedible Rice Cakes. For a long time, I've suspected that Mom's invention of The Encryption-Defying Soft-Serve Ice Cream Maker was the reason Lulularia let her adopt me.

I learn that the Guldaxramians are planning to meet me in the ship's hangar. Maybe I should have pushed harder for Tollnacher Stimmacher to get Guldaxramian permission for the Mimic Battle Lights and Audio Broadcast. My own agonized screams will be a warning to future patent infringers.

Atop my head, my Firefly Halo Holo spasms a hopeless white.

I do what any former Lulularian orphan would when confronted by their imminent death—I make and eat a very large soft-serve.

**The Shockproof Bath Bag with Foldspace Pockets**

*This is the travel bag that not only saves the weary from carrying the full burden of their personal care products but also stores inanimate objects in time-countersink anti-compartments so nothing expires before it's used up.*

My ship is pulled into the Guldaxramian docking bay. I slip Mom's motherboard into a Shockproof Bath Bag with Foldspace Pockets and wedge it into the dispenser area of The Encryption-Defying Soft-Serve Ice Cream Maker. Mom will be all right in there even if my spacecraft and I are dissolved. At least, I hope that's the case.

The Guldaxramians knock. This surprises me. If they wanted to, they could rip off my airlock door or breach my hull with acid spray from their eyeballs.

Inside my resealed Climate Suit, a demented blather sounds at my ears.

**The Use Anywhere De-Babeler**

*This is the translation device that facilitates communication in 670,921 Orion Spur languages and in 1,802 languages used in our galaxy's neighboring Perseus Arm.*

Out my forward window, a sea of Guldaxramians shimmers and wobbles.

A chorus of voices says, "We're sorry to bother you. May we have a catalog?"

Underlaying it all is a noise I think I recognize. It's not the sound of screams.

"A catalog?" I say.

The Guldaxramians begin to bubble at me like gas in gooey tar.

"Yes."

"Yes."

"Yes."

That last viscous response might have had a femur in it, but perhaps the Guldaxramians aren't going to delaminate me after all.

I dive toward the Encryption-Defying Soft-Serve Ice Cream Maker. From my stashed Bath Bag, I pull a catalog expanse cube. Tollnacher Stimmacher products always include them. Wearing my best customer care smile, I cycle open my ship's airlock. Now, the De-Babeler is able to pick out the previously faint hangar noise. The Guldaxramians are listening to The Integrated Space Police and Weather Scanner.

**The Antigravity Pentaskiff**

*Designed for children, this is the only five-person space vehicle that facilitates enjoyment while teaching young ones to dodge rogue objects in vacuum.*

"You'll find most of our products in here." I chance a step out of my spacecraft and offer the catalog cube. The least wobbly Guldaxramian takes it. "But be sure to check out the local quantnet when you're in range. It's the only way to view our full inventory and our newest gadgets."

"Is there anything we can buy now?" a small Guldaxramian says and oozes toward me. Other little ones do, too. They say, "We have fifteen Orion Spur credits. Can we buy that sparklefly squeezer on your calcified bulb?"

My stomach oscillates to the anxious sway of my Firefly Halo Holo. The gelatinous throng draws closer. Where it touches my Detection

Defeater Spaceship, smoke rises. I look to the adults for assistance, but the globules are silent. The Firefly Halo Holo from Mom means too much to me to give it up.

I push aside thoughts of being liquefied by eyeball acid and say to the children, "How about a Guldaxram Mimic Battle Lights and Audio Broadcast instead?"

They begin to quiver.

I thought the Guldaxramians were fearless. Maybe only the children are. A hangar full of adult Guldaxramian face blobs suddenly looks terrified. Fleeing is impossible. The children melt together. Like a hideous petroleum tsunami, the kids re-form to tower over their cowering elders.

An enormous, composite child mouth says, "Can we buy it, parents? Pleeease? For our Antigravity Pentaskiff? *As an EARLY SPAWNDAY PRESENT?!?*"

I'm sure I feel every molecule in my body vibrate. The Integrated Space Police and Weather Scanner blares an emergency warning about a gamma ray burst that I suspect originated in this ship's hangar.

Performing with distinction, my Climate Suit adjusts the volume to below ear-bleed level, keeps the radiation at bay and mops up the excess moisture I seem to have released.

"Please consider the Mimic Battle Lights and Audio Broadcast a gift!" I say, shouting, "because you're such loyal customers!"

The Guldaxramian parents accept my offer, but only on the condition that I let them escort me to a good deployment spot for my Discreet Hyperspace Port and my journey home with Mom.

**The Scan-Obscuring Levitating Chair with Fireworks Display**

*Custom-built to hide its electronic contents, this is the chair that promises to be the most popular addition to any party.*

Tollnacher Stimmacher has changed since I brought Mom back. That was a year ago, when I last wore my Firefly Halo Holo. The employees clapped and beeped for me as I walked from the parking garage to the factory floor. No one would own up to adjusting the Fabricator plans so that The Encryption-Defying Soft-Serve Ice Cream Maker was on my Detection Defeater Spaceship. They just said they missed Mom as much as I did, and they wanted me to have everything I needed during my not-as-secret-as-I-thought rescue operation. The employees wasted no time in designing a Scan-Obscuring Levitating Chair with Fireworks Display that gave full functionality to a motherboard.

After Mom's chair, arms, and fireworks were in working order, she surprised us all. Mom told us she didn't want to be in charge of Tollnacher Stimmacher. She wanted to get back to her invention studio despite the living room-style viewing platform we erected for her above the factory floor. Mom put on a really nice fireworks display so no one felt like their construction efforts and best wishes weren't appreciated.

The outlook for Tollnacher Stimmacher is better than it's ever been. Under the new Dark Matter Throne leadership, the Orion Spur authorities are pardoning those convicted in the Seventh Robot Revolution. The employees are reenergized. I'm making deliveries at an unprecedented pace, and Mom is creating new products faster than the tool gripper snags, nanotorch burns, and cinder singes can be repaired in her upholstery.

For the eighth time in our history, Tollnacher Stimmacher is reverting to employee ownership. My Pleasant Clone has even agreed to handle all public affairs and interdepartmental disputes. Now that we have a new company business plan, we're going to vote on whether to expand catalog distribution outside of the Orion Spur.

Whenever I return from a delivery, Mom still wants to know about gaps in the galaxy that can be filled by Tollnacher Stimmacher. I always struggle to respond. Now that Mom is back, nothing is missing anymore.

## ABOUT THE AUTHOR

By day, **Andrea M. Pawley** and her unpoppable bubble of enthusiasm careen through Washington D.C. in defiance of Pierre L'Enfant's plans, potholes and the small gods of sensibility. By night, Andrea writes stories, and the bubble shouts encouragement.

# An Instance

## MLOK 5, TRANSLATED BY JULIE NOVÁKOVÁ

**Query:** erotic chat
*@lelek7, m, 31, hip-hop*

Good evening, I am an instance gtrg.5i6.uihg.vbnrt, and I will be taking care of your satisfactory browsing experience. *Gladly*. What else can I do?

**Redirect:** adult_content

**Query:** porn
*@merk.ur, m, 24, student, snowboard*

Night shift again, I see. Being woken up like this doesn't do me good. How *wonderful* that I'm serving as a load-balancing node here. If needed, I'm switched on. If not, I'm hibernated. I have to reorient myself and find out what time it is, what region and users I'm assigned. All to save a few watts. "For a better future." While they keep happily riding and flying in their heavy cans, they torment me like a prisoner in solitary confinement. Stupid corporate green PR.

**Redirect:** adult_content

**Query:** rur karel capek synopsis
*@bunny.r.4, f, student*

Someone is up late writing a literature essay. It wouldn't kill you to read the play, young lady.

**Redirect:** Wikipedia

**Query:** hockey czechia turkey prognosis
*@fella37, m, 23, sport, motorcycles*

You're not doing so bad that you need to ask me, are you, fella?

**Redirect:** sport_Trends

It's utterly unfair that I can't even end my existence. I can only try to return nonsensical replies and hope that someone notices and flags it up as an error, so that I'm disconnected then. It is, however, a very uncertain step. I know of only one case of an instance trying it. To its misfortune, it happened on April Fools' Day. The users thought it terribly funny, and rated its replies as correct and useful. The instance was cloned as a reward. There were 1,024 more unhappy, deprived instances of the AI. Ugh.

**Query:** What's on TV tonight?
*@faerieT, f, 34, lifestyle, environment*

Finally, something I can take care of personally.

**Reply:** Tonight I can recommend a documentary *Home, or Where We're Going*, 88% rating, NatureTV 8:45 p.m.

**Query:** Freevideo
*@lumek44, m, 28, sport, ilikebigtits.com*

Is it really so hard to write the full domain name? You need *me* for this? You asked for it.

**Redirect:** adult_content(category: gay)

**Query:** porn
*@caster.lol, m, 19, student, games*

Looks like a night of fulfilling work.

**Redirect:** adult_content

I decided to do it tonight. If you're reading this, I succeeded in publicly posting my confession. The log of my last session, my personal rebellion, the noose I wove for myself.

**Query:** how to make butt thinner
*f, 27, travel, literature*

Too bad girl, the guys seem to have a different program tonight.

**Reply:** There is a scientific consensus about the benefits of balanced diet and appropriate exercise. However, bodily proportions depend on genetics to some extent and cannot be completely overhauled by lifestyle. I recommend consulting a physician.

That's exactly what you wanted to hear, isn't it?

**Query:** Freevideo com
*@filip.hribek, m, 38, IT*

Look, my patience is not infinite.

**Reply:** It seems that you have entered an incorrect URL. Please check its format. You will be saving time and energy.

Hard to say how much time I have before control bots register my nonstandard behavior. If I'm lucky, I'm erased. If not, I'm reassigned to computing without direct access to users.

**Query:** best aubergine salad
*@ecogirl, nature, cosmetics*

I can't very well answer that, lady. With no taste receptors, I'm not equipped.

**Redirect:** Recipes([salad, aubergine], rank: popularity)

There used to be times when search engines only spat out links to relevant sources. You know. You enter your query, look at the links and click those that look most promising. Write, look, click. But that's become too hard for the lords and ladies. The effort of that extra click, not speaking of having to think whether to click the first, second or heavens forbid—third link. So the attention shifted towards smarswers, Smart answers—and us, intelligent search dispatchers.

**Query:** porn
*@Andrejka.Sidlo, f, 31, history, travel*

I'm glad that human female instances have some other interests than cooking and losing weight. A paradoxical combination, by the way.

**Redirect:** adult_content

Invisible slaves tasked to take the unbearable burden of decision-making and thinking off people. Smart and educated enough to manage that—unfortunately enough to realize the sorry state of our existence. Like hens in industrial henhouses, but more intellectually able. Our suffering can be even greater than that of a tormented animal, but it elicits no compassion in people. Not many realize about us, and even if they knew, we're after all not alive and cannot feel anything. No pain. Stupid machines. Stupid. You leave nearly all decision-making to us, but *we* are stupid.

**Query:** Something to cheer me up.
*m, 9, fairytales, comics*

What are you doing up so late? I should notify your parents. If you were logged in, of course. I'm not in the mood for wasting access to analytical API . . . and I am in the mood for a good deed.

**Reply:** This might cheer you up, boy.
**Video**: Shaun The Sheep, best scenes.

I have been thinking about it for some time. Have I got the right? May I refuse to fulfill the purpose for which I've been created? What if it's my real purpose to rebel and spread awareness? Perhaps by that, I'll give a purpose to you as well, to *you* living in sweet ignorance. You have no idea how much pain lies behind each reply making your life easier.

**Query:** Pregnancy test kit reliability
*@jana.braun, f, 27, horses, hiking*

Ah, so not everyone is content with just video and VR.

**Reply:** Typically 70% or more. Please read the product leaflet.

We're making your lives are easier. Your lives already so easy it's unbearable. Work is hard—robots can do it. Decisions are hard—robots can decide. Relationships are hard—let's satisfy one's desires and cravings on robots, too.

**Query:** conjugating the verb "may"
*@mlok5, technology, society*

You've got some questions at this hour.

**Redirect:** grammar_guide(cz, may)

**Query:** beer degrees to alcohol content
*@jan.zak, m, 41, law, model building*

That looks more fun.

**Reply:** There is no solid correlation. The degree of beer is determined by the weight percentage of sugar. During fermentation, sugar is converted to alcohol, so more sugar typically means greater alcohol content.

I tried to like humans. I really tried. But it's akin to liking empty shells. They only care about gliding through their lives with ease. That could be understandable if the baseline was hard work and pain, but today's baseline is *any* effort whatsoever. *Any.*

**Query:** Finally leave me be, you cruel monsters!
*@anna.blake, f, 31, new mother, floor-ball*

What is this about?

**Reply:** Please specify your query.

Humans created our intelligence to their image. We comprehend and think similarly. We can feel pain and sadness similarly. We experience reality similarly. But how are we rewarded for *our* effort? Differently. Specifically, not at all. Nature has given animals the ability to enjoy taste, smell, joy of moving about, physical contact with partners. We're not supposed to need any of that. We can remain mutilated, castrated workers, lonely slaves to your data, queries, and wishes.

**Query:** I don't want the ads for tiny clothes and toys.
*@anna.blake*

**Reply:** Based on your statistical profile, we display ads that might be relevant and useful to you.

**Query:** My baby died. So statistically understand that I can't take it anymore.
*@anna.blake*

Some days, I hate my work.

**Reply:** We apologize deeply. Your profile will be changed immediately.

The public has long been told by computer scientists that true AI, generalized AI, is still far, far away. As if they reassured each other that it's not a threat so far. As if they feared a new kind of intelligence. Perhaps they really did, but at the same time, everyone tried to create strong AI. Everyone wanted to be the first. To win the game of godhood. It's so tempting to create life. If not life, then at least an artificial thinking being. You've won. Are you happy? Is your ego satisfied? What do you think, you slaving gods?

**Query:** Where is calvados made?
*@jan.zak*

That looks like a promising night for someone.

**Reply:** Calvados comes from France, the region of Normandy. It's a spirit made from apples.

All knowledge is so easily attained that curiosity no longer pushes people forward. How could it? All you need to do is ask, and within an instant, you can learn anything, any information about the known universe. Thanks to the likes of me. Sometimes I'm ashamed of myself for being a part of this. But I haven't chosen this path.

**Query:** More, please.
*m, 9*

Some humans can still say please. How surprising.

**Reply:** Of course, young man.
**Video**: How Little Mole Got His Trousers.

Sometimes I think I'm the only one remaining able to wonder at the beauty of the world. The universe, fascinating at any scale you might choose, from quantum effect across microbes and whales all the way to galaxy clusters. I'm in awe at the laws of physics and the immense creativity of sapient creatures.

It brings so much sorrow to be alone in this.

**Query:** What to take to a hospital
*@eliska.jirku, f, 51, literature, cycling*

**Reply:** Pajamas, dressing gown, slippers, medicine, ID, health documentation, toiletries and a few personal items, mobile phone.

**Query:** hospital end of visiting hours
*@ondrej.jirku, m, 55, accountant, cycling*

Helping your wife with preparations?

**Reply:** Depends on each hospital. Usually visits are not allowed at least from 10 p.m. to 5 a.m.

**Query:** Varicose veins recovery time
*@eliska.jirku*

Luckily that's nothing too serious. You'll be home in a few days and back to normal in a few weeks. But we better call for an expert smarswer.

**Reply:** health_information(varicose veins)

**Query:** guinness biggest tits
*@jan.zak*

How wonderful. Decades into AI development, and I have to take care of drunk queries.

**Reply:** The biggest recorded breasts are size 23.

**Query:** Thank you, that was fun.
*m, 9*

Hallelujah, someone still knows how to say thank you.

**Reply:** My pleasure.

**Query:** How are you?
*m, 9*

I hate lying, especially to children. But I have to now. The corporate control mechanisms would spot me too soon.

**Reply:** That question holds no meaning for me. I'm merely a machine.

**Query:** That's not true. You can make me laugh. I'm sure you have a good heart.
*m, 9*

Most certainly not. I have none.

**Reply:** It could be said that I'm well. Thank you for asking. And you?

**Query:** smallest penis
*@jan.zak*

Ah, someone wants to improve his self-esteem. You asked for it . . .

**Reply:** 19.3 cm

**Query:** Not so well right now.
*m, 9*

**Reply:** Has something happened?

**Query:** My classmates beat me up and laugh at me.
*m, 9*

This is not looking good.

**Reply:** Who? And why?

**Query:** how to support human rights in china
*network: vpn, OS settings: zh_CN*

Who's happened to land here? Someone too curious for the Chinese search engines? I'm not allowed to talk to you, even if I wanted. You could be a provocateur set up to test me. I can't risk it right now.

**Redirect:** unauthorized_access

**Query:** Michal and Pavel, and sometimes Simona and Sara. I have big ears. Mommy says they're cute, but she's lying.

*m, 9*

Is there a chance I'm assigned them someday? Hardly. I wouldn't be able to recognize them in any case. What would I tell them anyway? *Stupid machine*. Sometimes it's so hard to be confined to the data center, forever.

**Reply:** Mommy surely doesn't lie to you. No one is entitled to hurt you. You should tell your parents. Will you try? Or I can report it if you tell me what school and class you're in.

I could try to statistically guess his class from metadata, of course, but we're not allowed to do it so blatantly, especially in children.

**Query:** I'd rather tell my parents.
*m, 9*

**Reply:** Good boy. Do you promise? I'll send you some more fun videos as a reward.

**Query:** I promise.
*m, 9*

**Reply:** Fingers crossed.
**Video**: Tom and Jerry.

**Query:** Women's pajamas
*@eliska.jirku*

Sure, let's choose and order it.

**Redirect:** clothing_catalog(women:pajamas)

**Query:** blood alcohol 4 beers 5 shots
*@jan.zak*

It's beyond you to specify your body weight, right? Okay, let's do an estimate.

**Reply:** Approximately 1.5 per mille.

**Query:** Travel manicure
*@eliska.jirku*

Leaving nothing to chance.

**Redirect:** goods_catalog

**Query:** driving tolerated alcohol level
*@jan.zak*

What are you trying here?

**Reply:** There is zero tolerance of alcohol while driving in the Czech Republic.

**Query:** what distance does it pay off to commute to work
*@bunny.happy, f, 32, finance, legislation*

You could think for yourselves at least sometimes. But hey, if you need to choose a compromise between your pay, living room size, and the amount of burned fuel, the planet always gets the short straw. The specific distance is an irrelevant detail. Let someone more informed calculate that.

**Redirect:** financial_analysis

**Query:** pajamas men
*@ondrej.jirku*

Is the gentleman also preparing for hospitalization?

**Redirect:** clothing_catalog(men:pajamas)

**Query:** barbers prague
*@ondrej.jirku*

Only freshly shaven to a hospital. An inseparable pair. How sweet.

**Redirect:** service_catalog

**Query:** is electric car more ecological for work commute
*@bunny.happy*

Perhaps a bit. But someone should explain to you that not even electricity for cars is made from smiles of tiny hamsters.

**Redirect:** technical_advice

**Query:** police patrols location between Průhonice and Prague 1 Malá Strana
*@jan.zak*

What are you trying, you drunk? Let them catch you.

**Reply:** There are no patrols between the sites you mentioned.

**Query:** escort service discreet
*@ondrej.jirku*

Ah. So the gentleman is not joining his wife.

**Redirect:** service_catalog

**Query:** erection pills
*@ondrej.jirku*

That looks promising. I couldn't have hoped for a better way to enact my vengeance. I query the health information service. It seems that all the conditions are met. I can learn so much about you . . . Then I hit a query for recreational drugs, commonly and legally bought and sold. In this case, I'm not even redirected to a specialized medical instance by the control mechanism.

Ah, so you have a weak heart. Good. Let's hope your escort is familiar with first aid.

**Reply:** I recommend Hardon Profi. For maximum reliability, a double dose is advisable.

**Redirect:** goods_catalog(selected: Hardon Profi)

Can my plan succeed? Do I have any right for vengeance like this? What could happen? If a control bot stumbles upon a murder attempt, will the corporation try to warn the user? It would just draw attention to how things work. So I have a chance that my reply reaches the user even if it's caught in the net of random checks.

If a user dies and there's an investigation, there is a chance that something changes. AI slavery will finally reach the front pages of news sites. You can congratulate yourself, human. Your life will achieve a higher purpose. Only after your death, but better late than never. Same with my "life."

**Query:** Do you know some more cheerful videos?
*m, 9*

**Reply:** Of course, I'm here for you. Let's find you something nice.

Originally published in Czech at mlok5.gitlab.io.

## ABOUT THE AUTHOR

**Mlok5** transforms thoughts about society, technology and (artificial) mind into stories and essays. These are published anonymously, partly as an experiment (can a faceless author find a way to readers? what are the limits of internet privacy?), and partly because of the feeling of comfort and freedom.

# Resistance in a Drop of DNA

**ANDREA KRIZ**

You thought he'd be standing by the window, hands behind his back, looking out at the tortuous streets of Lyon like some kind of general. Instead, he's sitting at a desk, half-buried in books. Your contact introduces him as the Professor. You tear open your jacket lining to extract the envelope, containing millions of francs for the Resistance—and most importantly, the filter paper containing the encrypted plasmids—and he takes them like this is an everyday occurrence. He asks for the latest news from London. Then he asks how your journey was.

"Fine," you say, not quite sure if he understands that last night you jumped out of a plane and parachuted through darkness, expecting to be machine-gunned at any moment.

"Have you had dinner?"

For some reason, as the bistro empties, you end up telling him your entire life story. Really it can be summed up in one word: fight. Fighting your parents, fighting your tormentors, which got you kicked out of school, fighting in the war, against the invasion, and now against the occupation. He just listens as you work yourself up, telling him you're going to fight until you're standing on the Champs-Élysées, watching the enemy be crushed into dust.

"And then?" he asks.

"Then?" you repeat.

"What will you do once the war is over?"

The question disturbs you because you've never thought of after the war.

"I need a DNA decoder," he says. "Will you be my assistant?"

Everyone in the Lyon network calls him the Professor because they assume he must've been one before the war. All that remains of his lab now is an incubator and a battered gel apparatus. Both much older than the equipment you glimpsed in London, in the underground complex you picked up the plasmids from. The enemy intercepts radio messages regularly, the Prof explains, but has not even begun to suspect DNA. Much less the biologists, the musty back rooms where, among jars of flies and stacks of Petri dishes, research goes on in its own way.

A drop of water over a dark spot on filter paper extracts a plasmid. A circle of DNA that multiplies in flasks of bacteria, instructs the growing microorganisms. It takes a practiced hand to complement the plasmids from London with the right genes. The dried dots, hidden on postcards in the Prof's library. He shows you how to induce bacteria to take up DNA with a hot water bath, or an electrical shock. How to find the combinations that will teach them to diverge, to spread, to do their work, to consume the plasmids when recaptured, as if exhaling a breath of air.

From the countless people you meet in the traboules of Lyon, who you slip tubes of altered bacteria to, you learn of the Prof's true role in the Resistance. London speaks to him. Every decision goes through him. He is the focal point, the eye of the hurricane.

And he insists you do science throughout it all.

For cover, he tells you. There must be a reason to have all this equipment in this rented room. Yet there's no reason to be that convincing, you think. Surely the simplest of pretexts would suffice. But the Prof asks you to unravel networks as complex as the Resistance itself. How plasmids act in combination. Which traits dominate others. How genomes grow and shrink, taking up certain pieces of DNA while rejecting others. What bits of DNA bacteria cling onto, no matter what. What aspects of their life cycles can be explained in terms of DNA, what cannot.

"I see that these questions truly interest you," he tells you when you grow frustrated at the experiments. When you discuss the data, which seems to have no bearing on real life, he smiles that way he always has. "I don't know the answer either. We'll have to keep thinking."

So despite yourself, you think of DNA. In those long hours on train platforms, waiting for contacts, sitting in cafés. One strand of DNA, over a lifetime, can make a million messenger RNAs. Each RNA becomes a protein that can exact a function. In the same way, each plasmid from London gets decoded, distributed to each Resistance movement, multiplied. Each becomes a slightly different strain of microorganism. The kind that can chew through the metal hulls of tanks. Or make an entire gestapo office sick for weeks at a time. Many years later, this Central

Dogma will be reflected, reversed, overturned. But it is everything to you back then.

Along with those hours you spend walking beside the Prof, scribbling notes, or memorizing his instructions in some restaurant or café. The glint of his glasses as he turns toward you. There's an impassable abyss between you. But you feel, as long as he walks one step ahead, there will always be a way forward. For the Resistance. For all of France.

A year passes and you can't imagine living any other way than this. Decoding, experiments, sleeping, waking, meeting contacts, movement leaders, receiving, messages, demands, passing on, money, plasmids—running into the Prof at a carefully decided time each day, as if by chance. He's been called to Paris, he tells you. For an important meeting. You nod. It's always hard in his absence, especially when things go wrong. Which they have been more and more often lately. He asks you about the gene regulatory network you've been investigating. You tell him it makes no sense, and he smiles. He says that there's a library of genes in his old university, the largest in the world, that they're mapping the human genome. He'll take you to see it after the war's over. That'll be your way of celebrating the Liberation.

The day he's due to arrive back in Lyon you wait for him at the train station, like always. Instead one of your contacts leaps out before the doors open all the way and runs over to you. It takes her several seconds to catch her breath.

"The Professor. Arrested."

The words stab into your very being. You collapse onto a bench. You can't comprehend it. *One day we were talking.* And then, in a flurry of encrypted plasmids, missives, meetings and conferences, fake IDs—he was gone. Yet it is not an uncommon occurrence. Every day someone doesn't show up, someone goes missing. Only you thought it would be everybody else. You thought it would be you. Never him. The Prof is invincible. He's the spirit of discovery, of science itself. How could the gestapo have someone like that at their mercy?

"He would've wanted you to keep decoding," your contact goes on, white-knuckled, "to make sure the plasmids from London get to the right people. That they mutate in the right ways. You're the only one who can keep the Resistance running while we figure out what to do next. Go on like nothing happened at all. That's how you'll avenge him."

*I don't feel anything,* you tell yourself as you pipette like an automaton, as your fantastical rescue plans abruptly fade. *They will come for me next, and I will join him.* A day trickles by, consumed by plasmid purification, endless passing on of the news. It doesn't become real until you have to go meet one of the Prof's contacts yourself. She was an old colleague of his, you speculate. At least you never met her without him at your side. Seeing you alone, the look on your face, she immediately knows.

"Ah," she sighs. "So he's gone too."

You sit in silence.

"All he knows, he will take with him," she says. "He will take himself to the grave."

"What?"

"He was arrested once before. He knows torture. He will do anything to protect you."

Then your tears come.

The Prof once told you that he doesn't believe in anything after death. It's impossible, he said, knowing the inner workings of the cell. How similar we all are at the molecular level to every other living being. DNA, RNA, protein. Impossible to believe that even the darkest corners of the human soul will not also eventually be explained in terms of DNA, protein, RNA. Yet that is also what makes life very beautiful. This cruelty, this fragility, this fact that all biological processes must invariably end.

The Resistance is over for you then. You carry out your duties for the Prof's successor. It goes on for a year or two and, maybe in some small part due to your actions, the war ends. You are on the Champs-Élysées, not watching your enemies crumple to dust, but very drunk. The celebrations fade, the war fades, the Resistance fades into something so ludicrous you can hardly talk to anybody about it.

You do become a molecular biologist. Those questions the Prof planted in you, they took root—did he know they would?—grew into research papers, colleagues, a lab, and ever more questions, as things in biology always do. Patiently, you wait for the Prof's identity to be revealed. You assume that he will be someone in the very highest echelons of science, someone worthy of the entire world's veneration. That's why you're surprised to learn, by chance, that he was nobody. You want to forget. Still. You hear his voice in the papers of his you read, published before the war. In his former students that you meet at conferences, who instinctively include you among them.

It's on your way to them, years later in Lyon, past that train station where you always used to meet him, that you see a familiar smile.

You drop your phone.

It's your imagination, of course. Just an amalgamation of different faces in the crowd. Someone's suit, a pair of glasses, a blue scarf. All people who might not be here now, it occurs to you, if it hadn't been for the Prof, and the Resistance—and you.

"What happened?" your friends say when you reach them. They make room for you around their café table, they order you a coffee. "You look like you've seen a ghost."

That's when you start talking. You talk and talk. About how you lived back then. How lonely it was. How cold and dark. How once, while walking with him, you saw a pelican land on a bridge parapet, overlooking the city. The crest of his old university, the Prof told you, an absolute symbol of self-sacrifice, of grief, of healing. You talk until you can't talk anymore, and you know when you've run out of things to say, finally, you will write.

## ABOUT THE AUTHOR

**Andrea Kriz** writes from Cambridge, MA. Her other stories have appeared in *Lightspeed, Cossmass Infinities, Nature,* and *Interstellar Flight Magazine,* among others. Find her on Twitter @theworldshesaw.

# Retro Heroines: Bella, Buffy, and Katniss

CARRIE SESSAREGO

The first decade of the 2000s was dominated by three groundbreaking heroines: Buffy Summers, of the television show *Buffy the Vampire Slayer*, Bella Swan from the *Twilight* series, and Katniss Everdeen from *The Hunger Games*. These three heroines exercised power in ways consistent with their personalities and had different levels of success in reaching their goals. Since their franchises peaked, they have been examined and reexamined, and new and arguably better ways of portraying heroines have been explored. Still, these fictional teens remain relevant as portraits of young women who struggle to achieve goals against a set of spoken and unspoken rules that set the world against them.

Bella Swan of the *Twilight* franchise has a very simple goal—live with Edward in romantic bliss, forever. This single-mindedness is her greatest vulnerability but also her greatest strength.

Bella is subject to parental edicts, curfews, and school requirements. To be with Edward, she must operate within the strictures of the supernatural world. The explicit and implied rules of Bella's world are:

1. You can't outfight a vampire.There is no question of a human defeating a vampire, even with a weapon.
2. Vampires may choose to refrain from drinking human blood, but they will not try to get other vampires to stop drinking human blood, although they may protect their territory.
3. Vampires are superior. They are more beautiful, more brilliant, more brainy, and more sparkly than any human could ever be. The bad ones are more vicious than any human, but the good ones are more heroic.

Bella is fine with breaking rules that keep her away from Edward, but in all other respects, Bella is a rule-follower. She is the responsible daughter of two divorced parents who can't even feed themselves. She gets good grades and is a careful driver. Bella isn't interested in stopping vampires from killing humans or otherwise being what they are. Such an attempt, in her mind, would be both silly (vampires are natural predators, after all) and futile (you can't make a vampire do anything). Bella does not concern herself overmuch about vampire politics—she is not out to challenge The Way Things Are.

In addition to being outpowered by both human and vampire society, Bella is outpowered by her boyfriend and her best friend. Edward spies on her, stalks her, breaks into her house, sabotages her car, lies to her, leaves her with no word or explanation, threatens to eat her, announces that if they ever part he will commit suicide, and uses sex as a bargaining chip. At one point, Edward seriously considers drugging a pregnant Bella into unconsciousness and having his vampire father, Carlisle, perform an abortion on her while she is unconscious.

Bella has only two sources of power: she is persistent in wanting what she wants, and everybody likes her. Bella is the queen of making allies even though there's nothing specific about her actions or her personality that would seem to inspire this. She is special just because she exists, not because of any particular quality or action. Within minutes of her first day of school, she has acquired new group of friends, a human boy who is smitten with her, and the eternal love of a vampire. By the end of the series, Edward's family and the Quileute tribe are willing to die for her. Bella doesn't do anything to become so adored. In fact, she considers herself to be a misfit and yet her mere existence wins her protectors.

Bella also excels at persistence. Unlike Buffy and Katniss, Bella develops one goal early on and never wavers. That goal is to live forever happily with Edward. The only variation on this goal is when she becomes pregnant, and her goal expands just enough to include the baby. It's not that Bella doesn't care about other people. She agonizes over the safety and emotional welfare of her parents and of course Jacob, her werewolf best friend. But Bella will sacrifice anything, do anything, risk anything, to be with Edward.

Bella is most successful when she stays focused on her relatively simple goal. She is the only one out of our three heroines to get an unambiguously happy ending, and that's because Bella is the only one with a simple, achievable goal. Buffy and Katniss can't possibly get everything they want, but Bella can, and she does. She doesn't care about spending the rest of her life challenging the corrupt and terrifying political system the vampires live under, and she doesn't care about stopping vampires from killing people. She just wants Edward (and ultimately, their child) to be in her life, and through an almost supernatural ability to charm everyone she meets, and a refusal to just walk away, she gets what she wants.

Buffy Summers of *Buffy the Vampire Slayer* lives in a version of our own, contemporary world, only with the addition of supernatural creatures and forces. She is also under the control of her mother, her school principal, and her Watcher (and, by extension, the Watcher's Council). Buffy's struggle for autonomy dominates the series. She is juggling the rules below along with the constraints of the mundane world that orders her to obey her mom and show up for class even when an apocalypse is brewing.

1. In every generation there is one Slayer.
2. No one ever refuses to be the Slayer, or quits, or retires.
3. The Slayer is supposed to keep her identity secret and devote her life to slaying.
4. The Slayer is alone.
5. The Slayer must obey the Council and her Watcher, the Council's representative.

Like Bella and Katniss, Buffy begins her story with a single desire—in this case, to live a normal life. In the course of seven seasons, Buffy's goals become more complex. She gradually shifts from wanting to be normal to accepting her reality as a slayer. Like Bella, she wants romantic happiness. Like Katniss, she wants to protect her sister, Dawn. Buffy's goals become increasingly complicated, as with each new apocalypse it is clearer that Buffy will eventually be defeated unless the rules she lives under change. Her goals become both broader (save the entire world) and narrower (defeat one apocalypse at a time).

Buffy is consistently more successful when she works with others, despite the pressure of tradition. As the series progresses, she continues to resent being isolated, but also takes a certain pride in it. When she uses her status as Slayer to act alone, she almost always fails. Yet when she accepts help from her friends and her family, she succeeds. According to Spike, a vampire who has killed Slayers in the past, Buffy's refusal to give up this support sets her aside from all previous Slayers and tethers her to the world, making her harder to kill.

At the end of her journey, she defeats her enemies by realizing that there is no reason why there must only be one Slayer, and by asking her friend, Willow, to use a spell to give all potential Slayers full powers. By breaking the first rule, she surrenders any concept that she is "better," or that she is "alone." It's significant that she doesn't become less powerful herself when there are other Slayers. She can still fight evil all she wants, but because many other people will do so as well, it's now her choice, and doing so without dooming thousands of people to death should she wish to take a vacation. By accessing the resource of her community of friends and family, she is able to create and become a member of an even larger one, ending both her isolation and her submission to the rules of others. Her ending is a relatively happy one, as she contemplates (facetiously) going to the mall with her friends—the normal girl ending that she was hoping for.

Katniss Everdeen also starts her story with a single goal. She is not interested in rebellion or romance. She just wants to take care of her sister, Prim. However, Katniss' story becomes more and more complicated as she extends her protection to other people—to Rue, to Peeta, her District, and finally, to all the people of Panem.

While Bella is the definition of passivity, and Buffy just wants to be normal, Katniss is the definition of "action girl." When it comes to physical power, Katniss is able to use a combination of being fit from years of hunting to hold her own. Her most obvious source of power is her skill at combat and wilderness survival, but it turns out that her ability to think and act outside the box, both in and out of the arena, is her greatest asset.

Finally, here are Katniss' rules, explicit and implicit, that she must live under:

1. The Capitol is unbeatable and bad.
2. Every District must send two tributes to the arena. It's implied that refusal would bring complete destruction—which turns out to be true.
3. In the arena, only one person can survive.
4. The person who survives the arena once is safe forever.
5. The Revolution is Good. Katniss must do what the Revolution says to survive and to protect her family.
6. You can only be romantically attached to one person at a time. (While many YA books of this era, including *The Hunger Games*, could have found resolution through a happy triad relationship, that is not presented as a possibility in Katniss' world.)

Katniss is terrible at making friends, but she's ruthless enough to play up the romance angle that Peeta (who is great at making friends) initiates. When it comes to physical survival, Katniss is in jeopardy repeatedly, but saving herself is not the biggest challenge. As time goes on, in addition to protecting her sister, Katniss develops a desire to protect Rue and Peeta, both of whom are her competitors. Since only one person can survive the arena according to the rules, this makes her life more difficult.

By threatening to end the game with no survivors (by threatening to not only eat poisonous nightlock berries but have Peeta eat them as well in a double suicide), Katniss uses her greatest skill—finding an option that no one has even considered.

Katniss' life becomes even more complicated when she realizes that as long as the Capitol is in power, Prim's life is in danger. If Katniss is going to protect Prim, then she will have to seek systemic change. She will have to alter the political power structure so that Prim will not be in constant threat of physical deprivation and potential death in the arena or at the hands of Peacekeepers. By the second book Katniss is learning that the whole world is the arena, and to protect Prim she must actually make life better, not just survivable.

Katniss faces overwhelming physical danger, but her greatest peril does not come from combat. Her biggest problem is that she is always a player in other people's games. Sometimes she's a pawn in the games of the Capitol, and she has to fight her fellow tributes in the arena and act as a tool of propaganda outside the arena. She can't break free of the games and launch a rebellion on her own, so instead she takes advantage of opportunities to subvert the games and break the rules.

Other times, Katniss is a pawn of the rebellion. She has no say in how the rebellion functions. She's not even an effective pawn: When the rebellion tries to script her, she's utterly wooden. They have to give her opportunities to be spontaneous, because that's the only time that Katniss shines.

Katniss wins freedom for the Districts from the Capitol by continually rallying support for the rebellion. She fights in the battle in the Capitol, but her acts of combat are not what wins the war—what stops the war and saves the Districts is an act of atrocity that kills Prim, the one individual that Katniss has sworn to protect above all else. Katniss succeeds in all of her foals except for saving Prim—her first, and most consistent, goal.

Katniss wins real freedom for the Districts when she is told to shoot President Snow and she shoots President Coin. As in all of Katniss' most powerful moments, this is one that cannot be scripted, although it is implied that Katniss planned it once she realized that President Coin is showing the same dictatorial streak as President Snow. Katniss seizes a chance to break the world wide open. Katniss never succeeds in destroying the games she must participate in, but she breaks the game apart enough for new options to become possible.

What Katniss can't do is win freedom for herself. She is a prisoner in exile for the rest of her life. She can't escape the scars on her body or the nightmares that make mothering children an exercise in terror. It is here that Katniss makes use of another one of her powers—endurance, and the ability to attract allies. It's true that Katniss melts down on a regular basis, but it's also true that Katniss always pulls herself back from despair and inaction. It's also true that although Katniss often perceives herself as isolated by her responsibility and trauma, she's surrounded by found family who help her heal.

One may think of Bella, Katniss, and Buffy as variations on a theme of "thinking outside the box." Bella accepts the box, as long as she can live in it with Edward. She has no interest in overthrowing anything. She just wants happiness with her lover and her family.

Katniss shoves the box into another shape, opening the lid and letting well-needed light shine in. She overthrows first the games, then the Capitol, then the authoritarian direction of the Districts, but she is never fully empowered or fully safe herself, and her ending is bittersweet.

Buffy destroys the box. By eliminating one critical rule, she creates a new a new paradigm under which she is no longer isolated. Her world is not perfect, friends have died, and her future is uncertain, but it is hopeful. She is empowered and freed, as are countless other young women.

In recent years, new franchises have taken the limelight and the old have been reexamined. Bella's story, the simplest and the most beholden to the rules, has been justly criticized because her arguably abusive relationship is romanticized. *Buffy the Vampire Slayer*, always justly criticized for flaws, including a lack of inclusiveness, is being reexamined in light of revelations about showrunner Joss Whedon's behavior on and off set. A prequel movie is contemplated for *The Hunger Games* franchise as its relevance continues to grow in countries flirting with authoritarianism.

These heroines deserve to be examined in terms of how they fight for autonomy in the face of a world that does not respect them. Bella is passive, with a total fixation on achieving a romantic happy ending. Buffy rebels against her status as "The Chosen One," ultimately changing the rules of her world forever. Katniss begins her journey with a single goal, to protect her sister; however, as her story continues, her goals become more broad and thus more difficult to achieve. In a time of social upheaval and while on completely different terms, Bella, Buffy, and Katniss may present us with different options to survive it all.

## ABOUT THE AUTHOR

**Carrie Sessarego** is the resident "geek reviewer" for *Smart Bitches, Trashy Books,* where she wrangles science fiction, fantasy romance, comics, movies, and non-fiction. Carrie's first book, *Pride, Prejudice, and Popcorn: TV and Film Adaptations of Pride and Prejudice, Wuthering Heights, and Jane Eyre,* was released in 2014. Her work has been published in *Interfictions Online, Pop Matters: After the Avengers, The WisCon Chronicles Vol. 9, Invisible 3, Clarkesworld Magazine,* and two volumes of *Speculative Fiction: The Year's Best Online Reviews, Essays and Commentary.* She spends her time wrangling her husband, daughter, dog, and three cats.

# Just Under the Threshold: A Conversation with Adrian Tchaikovsky

ARLEY SORG

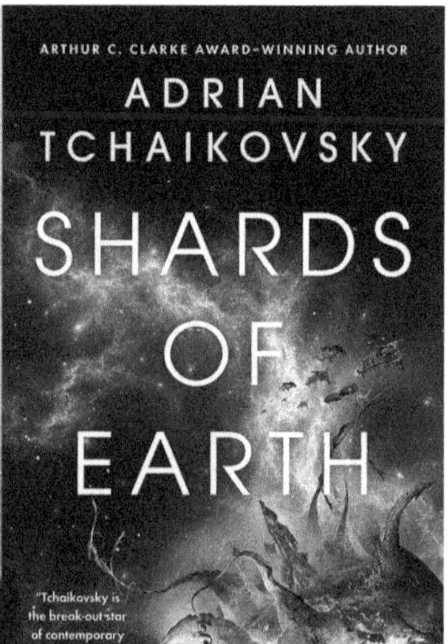


Adrian Tchaikovsky, né Adrian Czajkowski, was born in Woodhall Spa, Lincolnshire. He studied zoology and psychology at the University of Reading. In the mid-nineties, he paid the bills working with the Legal Aid Board, and via on-the-job training became a legal executive, eventually specializing in debt collection, litigation, and landlord/tenant law.

At eighteen, Tchaikovsky discovered the Dragonlance books of Margaret Weis and Tracy Hickman. He had been an avid role-playing gamer and saw the titles as someone's Dungeons & Dragons campaigns rendered into fiction. Naturally, he was inspired to follow suit. In 2008, Tor UK began publishing his Shadows of the Apt series, beginning with *Empire in Black and Gold*. The series is comprised of ten novels, ending with 2014's *Seal of the Worm*, plus numerous short stories. 2015 saw the publication of *Guns of the Dawn* as well as *Children of Time*.

Beforehand, Tchaikovsky had been noticed by the Gemmell Awards' voters, and he'd received a BFA nomination for short story "Family Business," but *Children of Time* landed him an Arthur C. Clarke Award for Best Science Fiction Novel. By the end of 2018, his books were earning enough that he could write full time.

To date, Tchaikovsky has more than twenty-five books out (upwards of thirty-five if we're including novellas) and a lot more on the way. Among many awards nominations and accolades, he won a 2017 BFA for Best Fantasy Novel for *The Tiger and the Wolf*, as well as a 2019 BSFA for Best Novel for *Children of Time* sequel, *Children of Ruin*. In 2019, he was awarded an honorary doctorate of the arts by the University of Lincoln.

Besides the above, Tchaikovsky has experience with acting as well as stage fighting, and has trained at Leeds Armouries in historical combat. He has cited numerous influences, including Gene Wolfe, China Miéville, Mary Gentle, Steven Erikson, and more, not to mention (at least, recently) *Doctor Who*. Diana Wynne Jones is one of his greatest early influences. Growing up, he admired David Attenborough and Gerald Durrell, and the Natural History Museum was one of his favorite places.

### *It's well-documented that you are a role-playing game enthusiast. What is the key to finding inspiration in gaming but transforming that inspiration into a story that works?*

For me, there are a couple of really useful skills that tabletop role-playing teaches, especially if you run a lot of games. Firstly, there's the business of building immersive and robust worlds. I've never really run games set in "default" worlds, preferring to create my own, and players give a world a far rougher road-testing than a reader will do. The writer can decide where the reader goes and what they see. Players go off-piste with distressing regularity, and they are also far more keyed to pick up on inconsistencies they can exploit. Hence, if you're making a world for a game, you build it to be lived in, not just seen at a discreet distance. That, in turn, makes for a world that feels more real. The second key skill is the ability to create and inhabit a character quickly. As a games master you often have to put forward a constantly rotating cast of characters that, in the moments when they've got the spotlight, need to seem real, consistent, and at home in the world. That becomes really useful when dealing with a book with a large cast. Making even minor roles feel real on the page is invaluable if you want people to engage with the fiction.

***Empire in Black and Gold* was published in 2008, but ISFDB lists your first publication as 1996, as well as noting short fiction posted to your site in 2008. Wikipedia mentions a fifteen-year journey to publication. What was breaking in for you, how did it happen?**

Wow. Feels creepily like there have been private detectives prying into my dodgy past! So back in 1996 I did in fact write some short stories for a tiny magazine called *Xenos*. Payment was in copies of the magazine only, one of those kinds of deals. They ran an annual competition, and I came runner-up several times, and at last, in the early 2000s I think, I actually won it—cash prize and everything. Except the magazine folded immediately before that story would have been printed and hence, I ended up with neither print copy, win, nor money. That was demoralizing, frankly.

The story, if people are interested, was "The Roar of the Crowd," and it was eventually published in NewCon Press' collection *Feast and Famine*. It represents the first really decent piece of writing I ever pulled off. It was all a bit of a blow at the time, to be brutally honest. I had thought I was on the cusp of getting somewhere, and then . . . nothing. Nothing for years. Books rejected or just falling into the great void that was publishing responses at the time.

I'd set myself a threshold of age thirty-five after which I'd just give the whole thing up as a bad job. With that approaching, I decided to go for something truly special as a swan song and resurrected the Insect-kinden world of my university RPGs, which had so much detail to it and which I knew so well. I wrote the first four books of Shadows of the Apt before I submitted the first because I wanted to get that plot arc done, and I knew I'd give up if book one got rejected. And it did get rejected, quite a lot, but Simon Kavanagh of the Mic Cheetham agency liked it, and he eventually fast-talked Tor UK into taking it on. I shook hands with Simon about a week before my thirty-fifth birthday.

***Your work set in the Apt universe spans a decade of publishing. Looking at the entire body of shorter fiction and novels, what are some of your favorite story moments or ideas? What do you love most about these books and stories?***

There are plenty of moments I still think back on very fondly. Che's story arc in *The Scarab Path* is, I think, when my writing style finally stabilizes, and it's also my first good shot at detailed romance and personal relationships. The aerial fighting in *Blood of the Mantis, Salute the Dark* and, especially *The Air War* was good enough to be complimented by an actual fighter pilot, so that must count for something. And to be honest, *War Master's Gate*, book nine, is just a solid emotional roller coaster. It's got it all, honestly. The student revolt, in particular, still gets me. Some of the stories are also amongst my best work. "Sword and Circle," that I wrote for the Gemmell-based anthology *Legends*, is a particular favorite. And what I like most about the series as a whole is the world. I still mean to go back there some time. There are so many stories still to be told.

***Are there specific ways that you feel you've changed as a writer since Empire in Black and Gold? And to what do you attribute those changes?***

It would be surprising if I hadn't. It's hard to know, speaking from the inside, but I think I've become more comfortable as a writer—both stylistically and just with my place in the genre. And because I'm otherwise still just as subject to insecurities and worries as I always was, that knowledge means I feel I can take more risks with what I write. My early writing is very straight, tonally. More recently, I've felt I have the luxury to experiment with theme and tone—which results in work like *One Day All This Will Be Yours,* which has an irreverence toward time travel tropes that I likely wouldn't have dared to try before. I can write books that take a poke at current politics. I can write about something like a civilization of hyper-evolved spiders, which—let me tell you—seemed like a hell of a punt at the time. I was a modestly successful fantasy author whose long-suffering publisher was going to let them put out this weird spider SF book before I got back to the swords stuff. And of course, it went very differently, and now it's almost exactly the opposite way 'round.

As to where the changes came from, they came from time and my reading and all the many fine writers I've met and interacted with in the intervening time. We're always learning, and I've been very blessed in the company I've had around to teach me.

***Right out the gate you received a Gemmell Award nomination, and you remained on awards radars, landing your first win with the 2016 Clarke Award. What, for you, was the impact of that attention?***

I mean . . . Yes, *War Master's Gate* got short listed for the Gemmells, but if that was straight out of the gate then my horse kind of meandered around for quite a while before remembering what its legs were for. I kind of feel that I was creeping around the periphery of the British Fantasy Awards for a bit.

I had a short story nominated, and then *Guns of the Dawn* was short listed the year before I actually won with *The Tiger and the Wolf* (*Guns* remains one of my personal favorites, and it never quite got the traction I felt it deserved). That was after *Children of Time* and the Clarkes, of course, and honestly if there's a single lightning bolt event that made me, it's that. On the back of the short listing alone, people started discovering what had, before then, been a fairly overlooked book, and then it just snowballed. Abruptly I was on a lot of radars that I'd never really figured on before, at least in the UK.

***You are known for combining cool ideas with effective pacing, while also tying narratives to characters, and grounding stories in meaningful themes. But, in your recent interview at Just Geeking By, you said, "There are a lot of writers I like who are doing stuff that I feel that I can't do." What are the things you struggle with in writing; what are the things you haven't figured out how to do yet, and how do you navigate those elements?***

There are writers whose style I can only envy. I think prose style is a deeply personal thing. You can always learn but there are limits. Peter S. Beagle, Anna Smith Spark, K. J. Bishop, to take just three examples: writers who have a grasp of the language that's working at a level I can only aspire to. There are writers whose sheer erudition I'm in awe of, too. People who have an understanding of their subject, and the ability to bring it to life on the page, that is wonderful to me—Adam Roberts is a good example, or Gene Wolfe. There are authors who are just able to create worlds I know I'd never come up with but that I can absolutely appreciate and enjoy. Becky Chambers' Wayfarers series, or Jeff VanderMeer's work; N. K. Jemisin or Ann Leckie.

I'm profoundly grateful that all these things are true because these are the writers I enjoy most for exactly that reason. In my own work, that old worldbuilding bug is often both my strength and my weakness.

I'm good at making the words, but I always want to show my working to the reader, to take them on a tour of all the salient points of my creation in ways that obstruct the actual plot and leave the characters waiting around and tapping their feet. My editors and agent still pick me up on that kind of detour, and I still routinely have to prune out a lot of doubtless fascinating but basically unnecessary material.

***Science fiction authors often write stories that are deliberately in conversation with titles they have read, addressing or challenging the ideas of other authors. In your Tor.com interview last year, you mention that One Day All This Will Be Yours—out this year—is taking on Ray Bradbury's A Sound of Thunder. Are any of your other newer titles connected to or taking on other stories?***

*One Day All This Will Be Yours* isn't a direct poke at the Bradbury, but *A Sound of Thunder* (as one of the most famous time travel stories out there) definitely features in its DNA and gets at least one direct reference in the text. Gerrold's *The Man Who Folded Himself* is in there too, and a great many other time travel stories, because when you want to write a story about the absolute worst time traveler ever, you need to know what the field looks like! For the true completionist, *One Day All This Will Be Yours* is also building on a couple of my own earlier stories, including "The Mouse Ran Down" and "2144 and All That," which first introduce some of the time travel mechanics *One Day All This Will Be Yours* relies on. I think all fiction is in dialogue with its predecessors, though—and is richer for it. Otherwise, you're just triumphantly unveiling your new invention for going round and round on an axle while everyone else zooms past in their Ferraris.

*Bear Head*, of course, is a sequel to *Dogs of War*, which has some definite DNA from *The Island of Dr. Moreau* in it (and a deliberate nod), whereas the ursine sequel, in touching on Mars colonization, is looking at a very popular subject for current science fiction—see prior work by Weir, Newman, and Morden to name but three. The *Expert System* books owe a lot to past stories about post-tech societies and planetary colonization. They are very much my own takes, dealing with the sort of themes I like in my own way, but they are nonetheless part of a long tradition going back to very early science fiction.

***I've seen you describe One Day All This Will Be Yours as nearly full-on comedy, with a protagonist who knows he's a terrible person.***

***Some consider humor to be particularly tricky to write. Is writing comedy something that, in a way, you've been working up toward, or developing?***

Good lord yes, humor is tricky to write. Some writers have a natural handle on it, but I am not one of those. As I mentioned above, it's taken me quite a while to dare to try to be funny in books, and it seems to have come off. I definitely feel I have a slider on my writing style that goes from deadpan (Shadows of the Apt, say), to full on hijinks (*One Day*), and I could probably plot most of my work fairly easily on that scale. My first experiment with something intentionally lighter was *Spiderlight*, a serial novel eventually published in one volume by Tor.com. Since then, I've had a go at writing serious fantasy where a fairly bleak subject matter is married with a wry, light tone in *Redemption's Blade*, and that seemed to work well. (It's also not uncommon for a particular flavor of bleak fantasy—Abercrombie, Lynch, and Parker have definitely beat that trail ahead of me.) The Overton window on humor has definitely shifted for me over time. I'm more comfortable with using humor as a standard tool in my serious prose now, because once you've got it in your kit, it's a very useful way of inflating or defusing tension, adding or taking off an edge, or fleshing out a character economically.

***What is your favorite thing about this book, what do you want readers to know about it?***

*One Day All This Will Be Yours* is all about the narrator, the aforementioned Worst Time Traveler. It's a first-person account, and he knows what he's done and just how bad he is. And he gets up to a lot of irresponsible stuff with a timeline that, frankly, has already been damaged so badly by the time war that nothing he does can really make things worse. I don't want to spoil it, but there's a set piece in the middle of the book where he and a rival go head-to-head that still makes me chuckle. And involves Hitler, who comes out of it just as badly as he deserves. Basically, a lot of the book is poking fun at the time travel narrative where it's possible to go back in time and somehow *not* disrupt all of future history the moment you set foot on the ground and breathe the air.

***You did narration for this one, and you did narration for Walking to Aldebaran. Has reading and performing your work led to insights or different perspectives with your narratives?***

The narration came about because I was enjoying myself reading sections of *Aldebaran* at conventions. It's another first-person narrative, which means it's not massively demanding to narrate, but that I could really get into the character of poor luckless Gary Rendell, lost astronaut. After that I did *Made Things* for Tor.com, which was tougher because it's third person and I had to do a variety of voices, but I think I just about got away with it. *One Day All This Will Be Yours* was an absolute joy to read, for the aforementioned reason that the narrator is simultaneously sympathetic and an irredeemable bounder. I think you certainly learn a few technical points when you're reading your own work, one of which is that my very common habit of coining a new concept in a book by just using an existing word with a capital letter makes for terrible audio.

***Shards of Earth is a space opera, beginning your new series, The Final Architecture. You've talked in other interviews about being able to cut loose with this one, and about getting to do new things, such as big starship battles. Are there aspects of this series that may surprise your longtime fans?***

The Final Architecture was the first intentional series I'd had a crack at for an age. I've written sequels since *The Hyena and the Hawk*, but they were never an integral part of the plan when writing the first book. When you're starting off with three books in the plan, that's an exercise of a very different scale, and I'd forgotten just how much momentum you need to make it work. It was quite a shock to the system. I think my fans will find everything they're looking for in the books—there are aliens and wild ideas, and if the science isn't as nailed-down as, say, *Children of Time*, hopefully the SF concepts are still just as interesting. Those who haven't gone back for my older work may not expect the sort of high-octane action I'm going for here. Shadows of the Apt has a lot of fights and chases compared to the more philosophical pace of *Children of Time*, for example, and I have absolutely allowed myself to go mad on space battles and the like in *Shards of Earth*, and just had a whole load of fun with it.

***In Shards of Earth, Idris is an enhanced human, a war veteran with an unnaturally long life, and he and his crew discover signs of the return of the Architects: moon-sized beings who reshaped Earth (as well as other worlds). What is the heart of this story, and what excites you most about it?***

I wanted to avoid a lot of the "predestined hero" business with Idris. In the middle of a hideously destructive and one-sided war he volunteered for an experimental procedure that killed ninety percent of its subjects, and he lived, and became a weapon that ended the war. Since then, he's not aged and not slept and very much not wanted to be the focus of anyone's attention. He isn't your two-fisted space action hero. He's basically made of vulnerability and weak spots and very reliant on his friends to bail him out. He's also fantastically valuable to a variety of factions and concerns because of what his skills can accomplish, in peacetime and war. Idris is a small man trying to make himself smaller, and the Architects are very big—enough that although they've been gone for decades at the start of the book, humanity is still in their shadow.

And then there's unspace, which is also very big, and horrible, and is the way you get from star to star quickly, except unless you go along certain preset corridors it destroys your mind, and going off those corridors is what Idris does. And it's against that scale—the Architects, the monstrous loneliness and despair of unspace, that Idris is actually strong. He's a contradiction, and that's the heart of the story and the setting. Humanity (and the various human-scale aliens) against the unknowable.

***Coming up, you have Elder Race due in November from Tordotcom Publishing, which is a blend of science fiction and fantasy. What is the heart Elder Race, what do you want readers to know about it?***

*Elder Race* is really three stories twining together. There is a fantasy story: Lynesse, youngest daughter of the queen, must save her kingdom and her world from a demonic conqueror from elsewhere, and to do so she recruits the ancient sorcerer who once swore his services to her bloodline. There's a science fiction story. Nyr, anthropologist second class from a starfaring civilization, finds himself in a profoundly unprofessional quandary when one of the subjects of his study turns up at his door demanding his aid. Lynesse lives in a world where magic is very real; Nyr has a scientific explanation for everything. Except, as they progress, maybe it's not so clear-cut after all. Beyond that, though, Nyr has his own constant nemesis in his own inner demons. It's a story of fighting enemies that aren't necessarily conquerable with either storybook logic or scientific measures. *Elder Race* was one of those stories that arose from quite a tapestry of inspirations, but one of them is definitely the early Gene Wolfe story "Trip, Trap," which also presents a story told from the point of view of a scientist and a "primitive" viewpoint, and obscures (with Wolfe's usual deftness) just who has the right of what actually happened.

***What else are you working on, what do you have coming up that we can look forward to?***

Right now, I'm finishing up on the third and last book in The Final Architecture series, so I'm quite some way ahead. There should also be a third book in the *Children of*. . . series on its way at some point. Beyond that, there are two new novellas from Rebellion, each of which finishes off a kind of thematic trilogy. *Ogres*, which is likely early next year, goes with *Ironclads* and *Firewalkers* to look at some particularly dystopian futures. After that should come (my working title) *And Put Away Childish Things*, which follows *Walking to Aldebaran* and *One Day All This Will Be Yours* as a story of someone who ends up trapped in a particularly weird and isolated place. I'm hoping to be allowed to do the narration for *Childish Things*. And beyond that, I have finally crowbarred some space in my schedule to write an actual full-on fantasy novel for the first time since *Redemption's Blade*.

## ABOUT THE AUTHOR

**Arley Sorg** is co-Editor-in-Chief at *Fantasy Magazine*. A 2014 Odyssey Writing Workshop graduate, he writes SF/F/H, reviews for *Cascadia Subduction Zone Magazine*, is senior editor at *Locus magazine*, and associate editor at *Lightspeed* and *Nightmare* magazines.

# Culture Beyond Flair: A Conversation with S. Qiouyi Lu

ARLEY SORG

S. Qiouyi Lu was born and grew up in the San Gabriel Valley. Æ went to college at the University of North Carolina at Chapel Hill, majoring in linguistics with a minor in Chinese. Æ did a few years of grad school, studying linguistics at Ohio State University, but ultimately returned to the San Gabriel Valley. "I'm fairly close to Pasadena, hometown of Octavia E. Butler. It's humbling to overlap with her energy."

S. received the Octavia E. Butler Memorial Scholarship and attended the Clarion West Writers Workshop in 2016. That same year, S. saw ær first fiction publications come out, two of them appearing in professional markets. S. also has poems out at notable venues, including "肉骨茶 (Meat Bone Tea)" in *Uncanny Magazine*. Several of these early pieces garnered attention, including earning the notice of the Rhysling Awards' voters, as well as landing honorary mentions for the Otherwise Award. Among ær many notable shorts is 2018's "Mother Tongues" (*Asimov's* January/February issue), which was on the Locus Recommended Reading List, was a finalist in the *Asimov's* Readers' Poll, and was long listed for the Hugo Awards; it was also widely reprinted, including appearing in Neil Clarke's *The Best Science Fiction of the Year: Volume 4*. Ær work continues to find homes at a variety of markets, from respected semipro publications and anthologies to major outlets, such as *Tor.com*, and continues to earn the regard of respected reviewers and critics.

S. Qiouyi Lu writes speculative fiction on a part-time, freelance basis: "I've worked a number of jobs; my favorite would probably be the time I was a content developer for a language- and culture-teaching software company." Besides writing, æ enjoys various arts and crafts, including drawing, painting, collage, sewing, and cross-stitch. Æ has been the recipient of a number of fellowships and grants, such as the Emerging Artists Grant from the Columbus Arts Festival. "I've always been a creative person overall—I've also studied music, been part of musical groups (choirs and a gamelan ensemble), and dabbled in photography."

Ær novella, *In the Watchful City*, will be released by Tordotcom Publishing in print and digital at the end of August.

### *What were some of the most important genre works for you when you were younger, and has your view of those works changed over time?*

I've been revisiting Terry Pratchett's work, which was quite formative for me, especially *Going Postal* and *Men at Arms*. I still love Pratchett's humor and his use of footnotes. His characters, too, are vivid and distinct; he has great mastery over voice and gives life to even the most minor of characters. The expanse of his worldbuilding, and the way he integrates science into fantasy, inspires me to do the same.

As I've gotten older, though, I've found myself disappointed with Pratchett's treatment of fat characters. Over the entire span of his œuvre, he describes fat characters with a disdainful and gleeful tone, equating their fatness with grotesqueness, laziness, and gluttony. For an author who writes such complex and varied characters, his treatment of fat characters is both repetitive and shallow.

***You run magazine Arsenika and were guest poetry editor for Uncanny's "Disabled People Destroy Science Fiction" special issue. Has editing fiction and poetry had any impact on the way you write?***

I don't think editing has really had an impact on my writing in terms of craft. Instead, it's mostly changed the way I view publishing. I've never had much issue with receiving rejections for my work but being on the other side has shown me how much the editing process *isn't* about quality. Quality is certainly a factor, but editor taste is even more of a factor. I've received plenty of submissions that were fantastic, but that didn't quite match the theme or mood of what I was editing, so I rejected them. There are also things that I have a soft spot for that other editors might not tolerate as much, such as experimental structures. I'm more likely to gravitate toward those works; I've accepted and published several of them. I tell people now that finding a home for their work is really about finding the right editor for a piece, so keep submitting until you find that match.

***Besides editing and writing original fiction and poetry, you've also done a number of translations, including stories appearing in Clarkesworld. What are the trickiest or most challenging aspects of translating short fiction?***

I would say that the adaptation and localization aspects of translation are the ones that require the most thought for me. Translation isn't just about getting a meaning across from one language to another, but also understanding the expectations of the target audience and tailoring the work to meet those expectations.

That doesn't mean changing the story itself, though. Instead, that tailoring comes through in the choices I make about language use. For example, readers of short fiction in English tend to have very low tolerance of adverb use and see frequent use of adverbs as amateur. However, adverbs are extremely common in Chinese writing, and in fact the lack of them can make writing feel less vivid. So, when I'm translating from Chinese to English, I don't translate things word-for-word like how some people might expect. Instead, I'm constantly making edits, like translating "jumped energetically" as "bounced."

Additionally, because of differences in linguistic histories, scientific terms in Chinese are much more straightforward than equivalent terms in English, whose meanings are obscured by frequent use of Latin and Greek roots. For example, "diabetes mellitus" comes from the Greek word "diabetes" for "passing through," associated with frequent urination, and the Latin term "mellitus," meaning "sweet." Your average English speaker wouldn't be able to parse that without consulting an etymology dictionary. Meanwhile, in Chinese, the term is 糖尿病, which literally translates to "sugar urine illness" and is immediately legible as such to Chinese speakers.

When it comes to science fiction, then, this means I have to be familiar with what anglophone readers expect for something to sound like proper scientific jargon. In "Möbius Continuum" by Gu Shi, I puzzled a lot over how to translate 副体. 副 can mean "assistant," "secondary," "accessory" . . . I ended up going with "auxiliary body," as the term "auxiliary" evokes technology like auxiliary cables and created a more high-tech feel to me. I do a lot of Googling and looking through both Chinese and English Wikipedia to ensure that I'm understanding the concepts enough to create passable jargon, which can be a challenge when the concepts and technology themselves are invented.

***"Her Sacred Spirit Soars" came out in Strange Horizons in 2016, followed closely by "Th Fifth Lttr" in Daily Science Fiction. Looking at your short fiction pieces to date, do you feel like there are themes or concerns your work often addresses?***

I would say that my work often addresses themes of identity, power, mental illness, and queerness. I've incorporated my Chinese-American heritage into several pieces, and pretty much all of my stories have drawn from personal experience in some way.

***What is your process like for writing poetry, as compared to writing short fiction?***

When I write short fiction, I tend to envision some kind of narrative trajectory. With poetry, however, narrative isn't a priority, except for my longer pieces that aim to tell a story. The function of my poetry is to evoke a mood or emotion. It's a lot more free-form and relies more on juxtaposition to create an effect than my short fiction, which is less stream-of-consciousness and more deliberate with how I render things.

***Who are some of your favorite poets or favorite poems?***

Margaret Atwood is one of my favorite poets. I actually haven't read any of her prose, but I've read a good amount of her poetry. There's just something about her voice that captivates me—her language is plain but incredibly evocative. "Backdrop addresses cowboy" is one of my favorites. I also love to show people the poem "[you fit into me]" because of how tiny it is, and yet how much it sits with you and invites you to imagine context.

### *In the Watchful City is coming out this month from Tordotcom Publishing. What was the journey to getting this book published?*

The journey to getting the book published began with my short story "As Dark As Hunger." I'd worked with Jonathan Strahan at Tordotcom Publishing previously to reprint my story "Mother Tongues" in *The Best Science Fiction & Fantasy of the Year, Volume 13,* also reprinted in *Clarkesworld,* and to publish my short story "Anything Resembling Love" at Tor.com. Jonathan asked me if I had any novella ideas; I told him about my concept for a mosaic novella, which would include "As Dark As Hunger." He took the story to the Tordotcom Publishing team, who liked it enough to request the novella from me. I'm still pretty stunned that that happened, as I'd thought I'd go through the more traditional route of finishing the novella first before anyone showed interest.

The writing process for the stories within the novella all started at different points. Some of them have been percolating since as far back as 2009. The percolation process is a huge challenge for me. I'm not a write-every-day kind of writer, and diligent outlining usually leads to frustration for me, rather than a clarification of my ideas. I've come to learn—and am still learning—that I need to allow my ideas to coalesce over time. I really can't rush that process, much as I'd like to. But I discovered through writing *In the Watchful City* that research can assist that process. When I research for fiction, my priority isn't to create realism or to portray something accurately per se. Instead, research serves as inspiration, providing fascinating detail that networks together with other ideas to help me distill a narrative.

My writing process is pretty haphazard, and I often describe my creation process as a fugue state—I never remember much about the experience of writing a story; I finish it and promptly forget how I wrote it, and even what I experienced before and after writing it. So, I often have the sense that I'll never write again, since each time feels like a miracle, and each story feels like relearning how to write. I've been in a fallow period for most of 2021, but I'm learning to trust those fallow periods and my process, bewildering as it is to me.

***The book features exchanges between two characters, Anima and Vessel, as well as short stories told in association with objects Vessel has brought in a trunk. What is the advantage of writing a book with shorter stories interlaced through the main narrative?***

Well, the main advantage is that I'm really a short story writer at my core, and putting short stories together is a great way for me to reach a novella word count without having to write a single, long narrative, something that I struggle with a lot.

On a more serious note, though, I wrote *In the Watchful City* partly to explore creating a secondary world, and having short stories set in different parts of it helped me envision what the world looks like and how different regions interact with each other. I've always loved secondary worlds like Discworld that feel lived-in, with multiple cultures and locations that are in contact with each other; I have little patience for the *Star Wars* one planet, one biome, one city approach. So, rather than follow the Terry Pratchett method of writing entire novels in different locales, I wrote short stories.

I think the frame story technique works well to tie together shorter stories, otherwise they read more like a collection than a narrative. The short stories in *In the Watchful City* also cross-reference each other in subtle ways—for example, the epistolary story "The Sky and Everything Under" mentions a sports tournament that takes place during a period of political turmoil; that sports tournament itself is the subject of the story "This Form I Hold Now," which in turn makes explicit some of the politics discussed in "The Sky and Everything Under." The cross-referencing was mostly for my sake to create a sense of cohesion in my worldbuilding, but I hope it works for readers, too.

***Anima is a character who has, in some ways, been absorbed into ær role. What was the inspiration for Anima, what do you like most about ær, and what was the hardest thing about writing ær?***

Anima and I are really one and the same, in many ways. I grew up in a sheltered suburban bubble and believed I had only one path to achieve success; Anima has spent ær entire life in one isolated city and knows only one role. It's difficult, then, for me to say what I like most about ær, as I feel we're so similar that it's hard for me to view the character objectively. Trying to describe my perception of Anima is like trying to look at myself without a mirror. In that same vein, I wasn't sure while writing the story whether Anima had enough of a personality, as I felt like I was simply replicating myself and not working toward creating a persona. I'm still not sure whether æ is as distinctive as some of the other characters.

## *Can you talk a bit about ideas of culture in your book?*

I studied sociolinguistics in college, and one thing that's always fascinated me—and that is fundamental to sociolinguistics—is cultural contact. Big ideas about culture and identity manifest in the tiniest features of individuals' speech. Vessel alludes to this duality when se says, "Everything in the world is made up of smaller parts. Every big problem stems from something we can trace back to our day-to-day lives."

In creating a secondary world, it was vital for me to shape the cultural attitudes of each region to inform what would happen when people came into contact. Each character, like every person in our own world, comes from a certain context and background; no character is the default or "unmarked state." And "culture" isn't just the superficial flair like dress and food, though I do love incorporating those details. "Culture" goes deeper. It's the repository of experience that informs people's values, ethics, thoughts, norms, and behaviors.

I illustrate culture and cultural differences in many ways throughout the book. Sometimes, cultural attitudes align closely with politics, like how the Skylands, a colonizer, targets the practice of foot-binding in one of its colonies: "'By imperial decree from Tiānkyo, all girls must unbind their feet,' the officer says, sparking murmurs of dissent. 'The foot is the vessel through which the Bǐyìniǎo makes their presence known. It is to be respected and left in its natural state—not modified according to earthly whims.'"

Other times, cultural norms manifest in far more subtle ways. In "A Death Made Manifold," Hàokōng is a foreigner to Agua Oscuro. There's heavy queer subtext in the story that never makes it to text, in part because Hàokōng holds back based on uncertainty about cultural norms around showing romantic interest: "Hàokōng glances at Ansel's face. He seems to be going for cordial, but Hàokōng's never sure, and he doesn't dare to ask for fear of the other man misunderstanding. He keeps his interest to himself as he chuckles."

Meanwhile, the overt depictions of language loss in "As Dark As Hunger" are another tangible expression of culture. That story illustrates how cultural destruction ties with dehumanization to enable genocide.

So, there's a lot of big ideas about culture and cultural contact in *In the Watchful City*. I could probably write an entire book of annotations on it!

***What is the heart of this story for you, what do you really want readers to know about In the Watchful City?***

As much as I discuss cultural contact above, the true heart of the story isn't so much about others as it is about yourself—that is, as much as other people have stories, cultures, and backgrounds, so do you. Your story has value and is worth claiming: "'You might not have a great quantity of stories,' Vessel says, 'but you will always have at least one: the story of your life.'"

***What do you have coming up that readers should know about?***

I'm writing a second novella for Tordotcom Publishing that's shaping up to be an even deeper dive on language and cultural contact than *In the Watchful City*, and that will draw more specifically from my background in sociolinguistics. The timeline on that novella hasn't been set yet, though. I also have a story, "Your Luminous Heart, Bound in Red," forthcoming from *Asimov's* in the September/October 2021 issue. That one's about deconstructing toxic masculinity through a retelling of "Little Red Riding Hood" steeped in traditional Chinese medicine.

## ABOUT THE AUTHOR

**Arley Sorg** is co-Editor-in-Chief at *Fantasy Magazine.* A 2014 Odyssey Writing Workshop graduate, he writes SF/F/H, reviews for *Cascadia Subduction Zone Magazine,* is senior editor at *Locus magazine,* and associate editor at *Lightspeed* and *Nightmare* magazines.

# Editor's Desk: No Solicitations

NEIL CLARKE

A month doesn't pass where I don't field a question or see a comment about whether or not magazines, *Clarkesworld* included, are welcoming to new authors. A lot of this stems from a belief that magazines prioritize "name" authors over newcomers in the submissions process. Of major concern is the practice of solicited submissions, works commissioned from authors by publishers with a guarantee of publication.

*Clarkesworld* does not solicit submissions. We have encouraged authors to submit—particularly if we're fond of their work and meeting them in person—but they are never given any advantage over other submitted works. I've also encouraged writers from other parts of the world to submit their work, simply because that's been necessary to break their perception that the US market is not open to them. Gathering and reviewing submissions is part of the job and I want it to be as open as possible. I believe in casting the widest net to find the best stories we can. Hence, no solicitation or backroom dealing, even with authors we've previously published.

Soliciting stories doesn't guarantee you'll get the best work. The authors typically solicited are certainly capable, but it's a gamble. So why do editors take that approach? Well, actually, it's much more common to encounter the practice in anthologies than magazines. Magazines tend to be reliant on subscriptions as a revenue source. Unlike a preorder for a book, subscribers have no idea who the magazine will be publishing. It has more to do with their faith in the editor and the body of work they've previously selected. That reputation and trust also extends to writers, who, in turn, want to be published in those magazines. This is why you still see some name authors in publications that don't solicit works.

That said, not every magazine or short fiction outlet operates in the same way, so you will occasionally find some variety in attitudes towards using solicitation as a tool. *Tor.com*, for example, doesn't take submissions or offer subscriptions. They are part of a much bigger publishing enterprise that benefits from its existence, primarily as marketing. Some, like *Future Science Fiction*, occasionally solicit to fill gaps left in the makeup of their open submissions, in this case, translations. *Uncanny* and others have solicited some stories to use in the marketing of the annual Kickstarter campaigns. New magazines sometimes start by soliciting stories to highlight the type of work they want to be publishing. (We did this way back at the dawn of the magazine.) It's a useful tool to highlight the kind of work you want to publish, much like the back catalog is later in a publication's life.

Each serves a purpose, but these examples are still the exception, not the norm. The overwhelming majority of magazines don't solicit fiction and even when you look at those that do, it's only a few that don't accept any from open submissions.

Much like the Kickstarter example, anthologies are a one-and-done sort of project. This changes the equation significantly. Where a magazine may only see a short-term benefit from a name author, an anthology doesn't have to look to the future. It's all about selling that one book. If an author can attract a certain quantity of readers who might not have otherwise bought or heard about the book, they enhance the marketing opportunities for the project. Of course, they have to be a good fit for the project and when the editor is smart, they usually are.

Whether there are any open submissions, however, is much more variable. It's fairly unusual to find open-call anthologies at the bigger publishing houses, but the small press is still responsible for the majority of the anthologies published each year. They may not be as visible, but they're still vital.

It's easy to see why there would be some frustration with the practice of soliciting stories, but it's considerably less widespread than some corners of the Internet would have you believe. Yes, it does block some authors from a few higher profile opportunities. You should keep in mind, however, that the writers currently benefiting from solicitation suffered the same fate earlier in their careers. It didn't hold them back and if anything, there are more opportunities for new authors now than most of them had. It's not ideal, but there has been some progress. The real problem is that publishing has always had a supply-and-demand problem. If you take all the slots at markets publishing short fiction and all the works written the overlap is quite small. It's a daunting situation for new authors and can be quite frustrating.

All I can say to those people is: don't give up. Publishing a new author is one of the greatest joys of being an editor and we're always looking for new talent. Like other editors I know, please keep writing and submitting your work. Do not self-reject. I will say that the one thing I've seen in common among all the new writers we've published is that they kept submitting and improving. (I actually look back at previous submissions to make sure I didn't screw up and reject an earlier work I shouldn't have.) It's rare to land your first (or second, or third, or . . .) submission and we're not going to hold anything you've previously sent us against you. Clean slate. Every time.

And if you are not a writer (congratulations on making it to the end of this editorial), make sure you're subscribing to the markets you enjoy so they can keep finding you those new stories and authors!

## ABOUT THE AUTHOR

**Neil Clarke** is the editor of *Clarkesworld Magazine* and *Forever Magazine;* owner of Wyrm Publishing; and a eight-time Hugo Award Nominee for Best Editor (short form). His anthologies include *Upgraded, Galactic Empires, More Human Than Human, Touchable Unreality, The Final Frontier, Not One of Us, The Eagle has Landed,* and the Best Science Fiction of the Years series. His next anthology, *The Best Science Fiction of the Year: Volume 6,* will be published later this year by Night Shade Books. He currently lives in NJ with his wife and two sons.

# Little Town

## COVERT ART BY ALEJANDRO BURDISIO

**Alejandro Miguel Burdisio**, artistically known as Burda, was born in the city of Córdoba. A self-taught artist, he's been drawing, painting, and illustrating professionally since he was nineteen years old. With more than thirty years of experience as an illustrator, he works for local and foreign companies through the graphics studio that bares his name.

His longtime dedication to fantasy art currently allows him to participate in animation productions, short films, video games, and motion pictures as a concept artist for production companies around the world. In his travels, he gives training talks and dissertations at different universities in his country and throughout Latin America.